# STORM

## SHADOWRIDGE GUARDIANS MC

### BOOK 9

## KATE OLIVER

# CONTENT WARNINGS

This book is a DD/lg romance. The MMC in this book is a Daddy Dom and the MFC identifies as a Little. This is an act of role-playing and/or a lifestyle dynamic between the characters and falls under the BDSM umbrella. This is a consensual power exchange relationship between adults. In this story there are spankings and discussions of other forms of discipline as well as heavy age play.

Please do not read this story if you find any of this to be disturbing or a trigger for you.

# ONE
## STORM

This was *it*.

Finally.

It had only taken him five long months to find the right one. Storm wasn't normally indecisive, but something about this had him tied in knots. Every time he walked into another showing, he found a reason to dislike the place—a crack in the foundation, a kitchen layout he couldn't stand, or just a vibe that felt... *off*. He'd started to wonder if he was sabotaging himself, finding excuses to avoid making an offer. But now, standing here, staring at the house before him, he knew he'd made the right choice.

It was time.

After living at the Shadowridge Guardians' compound since joining the club at eighteen, the walls had started closing in on him. He needed his own space, his own sanctuary. Otherwise, he'd never find peace again. The past year or so had been absolute chaos—squealing Littles, giggling Littles, crying Littles, stomping Littles, toys scattered everywhere, glitter explosions, and animated movies playing on a loop. The compound had transformed from a rugged clubhouse into a boisterous play space for grown women with pigtails and pacifiers.

He loved his brothers, loved what they'd built together, but it wasn't just *them* anymore. Their women—*their Littles* —had become permanent fixtures in the clubhouse. And with every laughter-filled movie night and every pastel-colored prank, Storm was reminded of one shitty truth: he was alone. And he always would be.

Swinging his leg over the seat of his Harley, Storm fastened his helmet on and took one last look at the house before heading to his realtor's office. The white exterior, the gray-blue shutters, the meticulously kept flower beds —it wasn't what he'd imagined himself choosing. It was so… traditional. The kind of house you'd expect to see on a cheery, festive postcard, complete with a golden retriever named Buddy and a smiling family hosting themed birthday parties on the front lawn.

None of those were in Storm's plans. He didn't do golden retrievers. He didn't do birthday parties. The flowers would be dead within a month of him moving in. And he sure as hell didn't do *family.*

But damn, if this house didn't feel *right.*

The moment he'd stepped through the front door, something had clicked into place. For the first time in months, he wasn't searching for flaws or picking apart the details. It was like this house was waiting for him, calling to him in a way that was impossible to ignore. He couldn't explain it, but the second he'd walked in, he knew it was his home.

As the roar of his Harley filled the quiet street, a spark of excitement shot through him—unfamiliar and almost jarring. He couldn't remember the last time he'd felt so hopeful. His breath was visible in the crisp air as he picked up speed, the icy wind biting at his skin. It was the kind of weather that would keep most riders off the road, their bikes stored away until the warmer months returned.

Not Storm.

Riding was his therapy, his escape. It always had been. Since the first day his dad had put him on his bike as a kid, nothing else had come close to giving him the same sense of freedom. While other people might pour their hearts out to therapists or write in journals, Storm let the rumble of the engine and the hum of the tires on the asphalt carry his thoughts away.

As he sped toward his realtor's office, the image of the house lingered in his mind. He could hardly believe he'd said yes to it.

Despite how brisk it was outside, people still wandered up and down Main Street, going in and out of diners, shops, and other businesses. That was the norm in the picturesque town of Shadowridge. A mix of tourists and locals were always buzzing about.

After finding a parking spot about a block from the real estate office, he hooked his helmet on the handlebar and put a quarter in the parking meter. A small kid with a blue cast on his right arm stopped in front of Storm, looking up at him in awe. The woman walking with him paused when the kid tugged on her hand.

"Wow," the boy breathed, his gaze fixed on Storm's Harley with wide-eyed awe.

The boy's mother, looking visibly tired, offered a weary smile as she ruffled his messy hair. "No motorcycles for you, sweetie. I barely survived you getting hurt on your *bicycle*. My heart can't handle something more powerful."

Storm's lips twitched as the scene tugged at a memory of his own childhood. His mom used to say things like that when he was a kid; her voice tinged with equal parts exasperation and love. He still felt a twinge of guilt when he thought about how daring—and reckless—he'd been. Broken bones, scrapes, bruises; he'd had more than his fair share growing up. It was a miracle she hadn't wrapped him in bubble wrap or suffered a heart attack from the stress. By the time he hit his teenage years, though, she'd given up trying to rein him in, finally accepting her son's need for adrenaline.

Still, as he got older, Storm had noticed that his need for the rush was fading. It wasn't gone entirely, but it didn't burn as brightly as it once had.

"I like your motorcycle," the boy said, his gaze glued to the shiny black paint and chrome, his voice filled with wonder.

"Thanks," Storm replied, reaching into his saddlebag. From inside, he pulled out a small, brown stuffed bear, one of many he and his brothers carried for situations just like this. He crouched slightly, extending the toy toward the boy. "Here. This little guy needs a new friend."

The boy's face lit up with pure joy as he accepted the bear with his uninjured arm, cradling it like treasure. He looked up at Storm, his expression a mix of blind adoration and gratitude that made the biker's chest tighten. It was damn cute. Despite the boy's mother's protests, Storm was certain this kid would be tearing through town on his own bike in the future.

"Say thank you," the woman prompted, nudging her son gently.

The boy's toothless grin spread wide, lighting up his face. "Thanks. One day, I'm going to be like you."

Storm grunted, caught off guard by the declaration, and shot an apologetic smile at the mother, who was now glaring daggers at him. Whoops.

"You make sure you listen to your mom, okay, bud?" Storm said, softer this time as he ruffled the boy's hair.

The kid glanced up at her and nodded earnestly. "I will."

Before the mother could fix him with another scathing look, Storm straightened and strode away, leaving the duo behind. He'd done his good deed for the day. Giving away the stuffed bears always left him with a quiet sense of satisfaction. For all his gruffness, he liked seeing people smile, especially Littles and kids.

As he pushed open the door to the real estate office, a soft chime sounded. He stepped inside just as a woman behind the desk lifted her head; a sticky note stuck squarely to her forehead. She blinked groggily, swiping at it clumsily until it fluttered to the desk.

*Had she been napping?*

"H-hi, sorry," she stammered, her voice soft and sweet. It sent an unexpected jolt through him, a feeling he hadn't experienced in ages.

*Jesus, when's the last time my cock reacted to a voice?*

"I thought I'd locked the door," she added.

"Are you closed?" he snapped, his tone sharper than he intended.

*Whoa. Okay. Dial it back. Don't be a dick just because she's got you rattled.*

Her wide-set eyes roamed up his body, taking him in from his boots to his leather jacket, pausing at his chest before finally meeting his gaze. She nibbled on her bottom lip, her expression caught somewhere between nervous and flustered. When their eyes locked, her mouth fell open slightly, and the tension in the room crackled with static electricity.

"No," she managed barely above a whisper. "I mean, sort of. It's my lunch break, and no one else is in the office right now, so I usually lock the door during that time."

He tilted his head, his dark eyes narrowing slightly. "There's no lunch on your desk."

Her cheeks flushed a rosy pink, the color creeping down her neck as she brought her hands—delicate and painted a soft blush—to cover her face. And just like that, his mind derailed. All he could think about was those tiny hands wrapped around his cock.

*Jesus Christ. What the fuck is wrong with me?*

He clenched his jaw, forcing himself to focus.

*Get it together, asshole.*

"A short nap seemed more appealing." She giggled, her soft laughter a quiet ripple that seemed to hang in the air. "What can I help you with?"

Storm frowned, watching her closely. The dark circles under her eyes stood out against her otherwise smooth, porcelain skin.

*Why is she so tired?* The thought nagged at him. *Is she skipping lunch, too? Fuck, why do I care?*

"I'm supposed to meet Charlie here to work up an offer on a house," he said, his voice was still harsher than he meant.

She nodded, and as her chestnut-brown hair swished, a glint of something sparkly caught his eye—a pink barrette nestled in her waves. It was such a small, whimsical detail, yet it felt oddly significant. She clearly liked pink. His mind flicked to the Littles at the Guardians' compound. The barrette and her demeanor reminded him of them.

His brow arched slightly as the thought crossed his mind. Could she be Little? Lots of grown women liked pink without it meaning anything more.

*It doesn't matter anyway.*

If he wanted to play Daddy, he'd go to a club. No strings. No emotions. Just a night to be slightly less grumpy. That's all he was good for. Women didn't like men like him long term; they never would. His personality wasn't exactly going to win him any popularity contests.

"Oh, well, if you'd like to sit and wait, I'm sure he'll be here shortly," she chirped, gesturing toward a small cluster of furniture a few feet away from her desk.

Her polite cheer made irritation prickle at the back of his neck. He hated waiting, but Charlie knew he was coming, so surely, he'd show up soon. Storm let out a heavy sigh and sank onto one of the chairs, his broad frame dwarfing the sleek, modern furniture. From his seat, he watched as the receptionist shuffled papers, tapping at her computer like she was trying to look busy.

A minute passed. Then another.

"Why are you so tired?" he asked abruptly, the question slipping out before he could stop it.

She startled, her head snapping up as her cheeks flushed a somehow deeper shade. "Late night," she replied with a small shrug, her tone nonchalant.

Late doing what? Partying, probably. She looked to be in her twenties, the prime age for wild nights and crowded clubs. Storm wouldn't know. Partying had never been his thing. Too many people, too much noise.

Before he could ask anything else, the door opened, and Charlie strode in. "Storm, sorry to make you wait. I got caught in traffic. Come on back to my office."

Storm rose, following Charlie toward his office, but not before casting one last glance at the receptionist. She avoided his gaze, her attention fixed on her desk, which only served to annoy him further. What was it about her that made him feel so uneasy? He couldn't remember the last time a woman had rattled him like this.

As they passed her, Storm adjusted his jeans discreetly, cursing under his breath. His body's reaction to her presence was undeniable and frustrating as hell.

"So, you're ready to make the vendor an offer?" Charlie asked as they entered his small office. "I have to say, I'm surprised you decided on this house. I mostly sent you there because I didn't have much else to show at the time."

"Offer twenty over asking," Storm said flatly, sitting on the chair across from Charlie's desk. "And ask for an expedited closing date."

Charlie raised an eyebrow, his fingers hovering over the keyboard. "That's pretty aggressive. Sure about that?"

Storm shot him a sharp look, and Charlie chuckled

nervously before typing again. Storm wasn't the type of man people figured out easily. Hell, half the time, he didn't even understand who he was himself. Maybe that's why he fitted in so well with the MC. The club was a family of misfits, each man different but bound together by something unshakable.

An hour later, Storm emerged from Charlie's office, marching toward the exit.

"Have a nice day," the receptionist called out cheerfully, her sweet voice like a balm against his in-built irritation.

He paused mid-stride, turning to look at her one last time. Those big doe eyes of hers blinked up at him, innocent and wide, and something inside him twisted painfully. He grunted a noncommittal response and stomped out the door.

*Never fucking coming back here again.*

The last thing he wanted was to see her again—those soft, pink lips, the way the blush crept up her neck, the sparkle in her hair. And yet, he had a sinking feeling that she'd be haunting him anyway—her image burned into his mind as he stroked himself later that night.

As his Harley roared to life, he let out an unsteady breath, stealing one last glance at the real estate office. His grip tightened on the handlebars.

*Best to stay far away from her.*

"Stormy-Normy's home!" Ivy squealed, as usual she was full of mischief as she twirled in place, her pink tutu flaring out dramatically. The sparkly princess crown perched on her head tilted precariously with the movement, but she didn't seem to care.

Storm scowled, his dark gaze settling on the sassy Little girl. She stood there with her hands on her hips, her tutu puffed out like a cotton-candy cloud. They must've been playing dress-up again, though it wasn't exactly unusual for the Littles to prance around in tutus and crowns for no reason at all.

"Don't call me that," he snapped.

Ivy giggled, completely unfazed by his gruffness. None of the girls ever took him seriously, no matter how hard he tried. They all deserved their bottoms spanked more often, in his opinion. Not that it would stop them; if anything, they seemed to *enjoy* getting into trouble. Mischief was practically their lifeblood.

"Why not? It's cute," Ivy shot back, her pout exaggerated for effect. "You call me Sprite."

Storm glared at her, his lips twitching against a smile he refused to let show. He reached out and tapped her nose lightly, eliciting another giggle from Ivy. "That's because you're small."

"Well, if you don't want me to call you Stormy-Normy —which, by the way, is *pretty dang clever*—what *do* you want me to call you?" Ivy tilted her head, her crown slipping slightly as her wide eyes sparkled with mock innocence.

"Storm," he replied bluntly. "That's my name."

He headed for the fridge for a beer, grabbing a second

bottle just as Kade and Remi strolled into the common area. Kade snatched one of them out of Storm's hand with a casual grin, lifting his chin in reply.

"Thanks, man."

Across the room, Ivy and Remi hugged and squealed as if they hadn't seen each other in years, even though it had probably only been a few hours. It didn't matter how much time they spent apart; the Littles acted like every reunion was a heartfelt occasion. It was, admittedly, kind of cute. The entire MC functioned like a big, chaotic family, and the girls were no exception.

"Storm doesn't like his new nickname," Ivy informed Remi, her tone conspiratorial.

Remi rolled her heavily lined eyes, the dramatic gesture offset by the bright pink bow perched on her head. Storm smirked internally at the sight. Remi's gothic style was legendary, but ever since she'd gotten together with Kade, she'd been embracing her secret love of pink in a way that was downright endearing. She still wore black, but the pops of color never failed to make him chuckle. It was *adorable*, not that he'd ever admit it.

"Of course he doesn't. Storm doesn't like *anything* fun," Remi muttered, crossing her arms with exaggerated exasperation.

The words hit harder than they should've. Storm's chest tightened, and he furrowed his brow. He wasn't *that* bad, was he? He liked fun—he was just out of practice. When was the last time he'd actually *enjoyed* something? Hell, had he always been this grumpy, or was it just his age catching up with him?

"I like fun," he growled, crossing his arms over his chest as his scowl deepened.

Both girls turned look at him, their smirks identical, full of bratty mischief. Little troublemakers.

"Yeah?" Ivy asked, her tone full of challenge. "So that means you're going to help us decorate for Carlee's birthday party tomorrow?"

Storm froze. *Fuck.* He'd forgotten about that. It felt like there was a birthday party every other week, one of the reasons he'd finally decided to buy a house of his own. The clubhouse was too much—too loud, too excited, too... *full.* The girls hyped up on cake and in full Little Space were pure chaos, and he usually hid in his small apartment until the sugar crash hit.

He glared at them, his scowl deepening. "No."

Then, without waiting for a response, he stomped off, muttering curses under his breath. Behind him, Ivy and Remi's giggles followed like a trail of sparkles.

"Love you, Stormy-Normy!" they called out in unison, their sing-song voices brimming with cheeky glee.

*Brats.* Storm shook his head, the faintest smile tugging at his lips despite himself.

"You're in a great mood. Remi's starting to think you hate her."

Storm paused mid-swipe, glancing up from the car part

in his hands as Kade approached, leaning his broad frame casually against one of the large toolboxes. His friend's tone was teasing, but there was an edge of seriousness beneath it. "That's ridiculous. You know I don't hate her," Storm muttered, then turned his focus back to wiping down the component from the classic Chevy Chevelle in front of him. The part gleamed under the overhead lights, but his mind wasn't on the task anymore.

"*I* know that," Kade replied, folding his arms, "but when all you do is snap at them, their Little hearts don't know that. It hurts their feelings."

*Shit.*

Storm's jaw tightened, and he stared at the metal in his hand, suddenly unable to concentrate. The last thing he ever wanted was to make any of the Littles sad. Sure, he wanted his own space, away from the chaos and noise, but that didn't mean he didn't care about them. Hell, he'd put his life on the line for any of them without hesitation. They were his family, too.

"You've been extra dickish lately," Kade added, his voice lighter but still pointed. "What's going on with you?"

Storm bristled at the comment but couldn't bring himself to deny it. If he was being honest *totally* honest he had been crankier than usual. But the cause? That was harder to pinpoint. It could be the lack of sex, but deep down, he wasn't convinced that was it.

"I'm not being extra *anything*," he snarled, though he hadn't meant it to come out like that.

Kade snorted, shaking his head. "Bullshit. I've known

you forever. You haven't been yourself. So, what the fuck is going on? Why are you so on edge?"

Storm sighed, setting the car part aside with a metallic *clink*. After tossing the oily rag over his shoulder, he turned to face his friend. Kade wasn't going to let this go, that much was clear.

"I'm buying a house." Storm's words were heavier than he'd expected. "I put in an offer on one today."

Kade's brows drew together as he studied him. "You've never talked about wanting to live outside the clubhouse. What's brought that on?"

Storm hesitated, unsure how to answer. He wasn't used to talking about his feelings, especially not when they felt so tangled. When he didn't respond right away, Kade let out a deep sigh.

"Does it have something to do with all the Littles we have around here now?" Kade asked bluntly.

Hearing it said out loud hit hard, making him feel like an asshole. Apparently, everyone already thought he was one anyway.

"It's a lot, being around them all the time," he said finally, the honesty sitting heavy on his chest.

"No shit," Kade said with a glimmer of humor. "They're fucking loud, bratty, and a total pain in the ass." His lips curved into a small smile. "But are you buying a house to get away from them or because being around them constantly reminds you of what you don't have?"

Storm's chest tightened at the question, something sharp twisting inside him. He met Kade's gaze but didn't have an answer. Or maybe he didn't *want* to have an answer.

"It's time for me to live on my own," he said gruffly. "Besides, the girls will be thrilled not to have me around, you know, being such an asshole."

Kade smirked and pushed off the toolbox. "Actually, I think they're going to be crushed that you're moving out. Like it or not, they love you—despite your sparkling personality."

Storm stared after him in stunned silence as Kade strode out of the garage, his words lingering like an echo in the air. *The girls love me?* That felt like a stretch. They tolerated him, teased him relentlessly, and harassed him on a regular basis. Surely, they weren't going to have a second thought to him leaving.

And yet, the idea of not seeing them every day made his stomach roil uncomfortably.

What the hell was that all about?

# TWO
## BROOK

What a day.

One of these days, Brook was going to learn. She was going to make the responsible choice. It probably wouldn't be today. And most likely not tomorrow, either. But one day, because eventually, these late nights would *really* catch up with her.

"Have a great night," she called out to the real estate agents she worked for.

"You too," one of them replied.

Oh, she would. It was going to be a fabulous evening. Her bathtub was calling her name. So was the chocolate she had stashed in her kitchen. Add in the book she'd been reading the night before that had just gotten to the good part and she was going to have the time of her life.

It was nearly dark when she parked in her designated spot in her apartment complex. She hated this time of year. That wasn't totally true. She didn't mind the winter. But the early darkness is what she didn't like. Which was why she ran from her car to her apartment and got herself inside as quickly as possible.

As soon as she had the door locked behind her, she let out a breath and kicked off her heels.

*Stupid grown-up shoes. I hate those things.*

Pretending to be an adult all day long was exhausting. Technically, she was an adult. By law, anyway. On the inside, she was anything but.

"Bubbles, Creamsicle, I'm home," she sang.

They didn't respond, of course. Well, in her mind, they did. But not out loud because that would be weird. They were stuffed toys, after all.

Deciding to take a bath first, she stripped out of her office clothes and turned on the water. As she waited for it to fill, her phone buzzed on the counter.

Carlee: You're still coming tomorrow, right?

She grinned and did a little naked wiggle. Of course she was still going to Carlee's birthday party. Not only was it a Littles party, but it was also at the motorcycle club compound where Carlee and her boyfriend lived. Brook had only been there a couple of times, but she always loved it. She had no idea why. Maybe it was because all the people she'd met there were so nice. Everyone Carlee had introduced her to had been friendly and welcoming, which wasn't something she had expected from a bunch of tatted-up bikers. She'd always tried to be non-judgmental but the first time she'd gone to visit her friend, Brook had been terrified. That only lasted about five minutes when one of the guys made them hot cocoa with extra whipped cream. Who could be scared of that? Not her.

> Brook: Of course. I can't wait.

Carlee: Yay!

Smiling, she poured in half a bottle of bubble bath into the water, then decided that wasn't enough, so she poured a bit more. Her entire bathroom smelled like bubble gum.

After dumping a bucket of toys into the tub, she lowered herself into the hot water and hummed. *Perfect.*

There wasn't anything Brook could think of that could make her life better. Well, maybe one thing. The problem was she was painfully introverted. Other than going to work every day, the only other places Brook went were the library and the grocery store. And occasionally to see Carlee. There was no doubt she would have to decompress for the rest of the weekend after her friend's birthday party tomorrow night. Thankfully, Carlee understood. Some people didn't, which was why she'd struggled to make friends. And finding a Daddy.

Oh well. She could be her own caregiver. That was a thing, right? She even had rules she'd come up with for herself. Not that she'd punished herself when she'd broken them. That would just be silly.

She stuck her tongue between her teeth as she twisted the bath mermaid's tail and then put her in the water to swim. When the doll swam into the mountain of foam, Brook grabbed her and did it again. When the water started to cool, she set her toys up on the ledge to dry and started washing herself.

By the time she had on a fresh pair of cotton panties and one of her pink frilly nightgowns that fell to her thighs, she was starving. She also wanted to watch an animated movie. And read. It didn't seem to matter how late she stayed up to read each night, her TBR list just kept getting longer and longer.

Brook shuffled through the fridge and cupboards, pulling out random things that looked good. Finger foods were her favorite. Utensils were overrated and a waste of time.

She made herself a charcuterie board of sorts, proud of herself by the time she was done. It was beautiful. And so delicious. She even put some greens on the plate. They were M&Ms, but still. They were green. There was also fruit in the Pop-Tart, protein in the peanut butter cups, and carbs in the mini-donuts. It was all around a well-balanced meal. In her eyes, at least. And she was her own caregiver, so hers was the only opinion that mattered.

Dinner in hand and a sippy cup of soda, Brook went into her bedroom and spent a few minutes nesting. Her room was her favorite place to be. Even though the entire apartment was hers, she still preferred to be in the smaller space rather than her living room. It was where she felt comfortable. It was also where all her toys and fun decorations were so it was easier to slip into Little Space there. She had hung some fairy lights around the top of the wall, and her bed had a cute canopy she'd seen and had to buy for herself. That was one of the benefits of being your own caregiver.

Once she had her pink-and-white bedding fluffed and

her bubblegum fuzzy blanket spread out, she settled in and found a movie to get lost in.

*Just one more chapter.*

Brook turned the page, trying her best to ignore the clock on the nightstand that told her that she was still reading in the wee hours of the morning. At least it was Friday, and she could spend all Saturday recovering from pulling three near-all-nighters this week. She blamed it on all the amazing books she couldn't get enough of. It was easy to get lost in those worlds and forget about real life. At least until her alarm sounded at six o'clock in the morning on workdays.

Her stomach gurgling in the dark, silent room nearly startled her. Except it had been doing that for the past couple of hours, and she was starting to think her dinner choice wasn't the best plan.

Three chapters later, Brook turned off her e-reader and went to the bathroom to find a ginger chew to settle her tummy. The last thing she needed was to be tired and feel like crap when she woke up.

Checking her phone to make sure the alarm was set, she groaned. She would only have about three hours to sleep. Good thing her job was pretty easy and it was the slow time of year for house buying. She just hoped the grumpy tattooed guy didn't come back in the next day, looking at her full of disapproval. It didn't matter that he was the best-looking man she'd ever seen. He was as prickly as a cactus and clearly disliked her.

She let out a sigh, ignoring the need to squeeze her thighs together from thinking about him, and hugged her stuffed elephant tightly.

"Night, Bubbles," she mumbled sleepily before she dozed off seconds later.

What had she been thinking?

Being in charge of herself was sometimes a major disadvantage. Especially when she got so absorbed in a book. Now, her entire Friday seemed to be lasting forever, and all she wanted to do was go home and take a nap. Except that wasn't going to happen because she had Carlee's birthday party to go to. Which she was excited for, actually. A Littles birthday party. Her friend was so lucky to have the life she did.

Brook knew how rare it was to find a good Daddy and be able to spend so much time in Little Space. Somehow, Carlee and all the other Littles in the MC had found that, but she wasn't hopeful for herself. She wasn't the typical Little. Loud noises and a lot of commotion exhausted her, so she could only be around it in small doses. A Daddy didn't want a Little who was an anti-social introvert. That went against everything a Little should be. At least, so she thought.

When five o'clock finally rolled around, she couldn't

get out of the office fast enough. It wasn't that she didn't love her job. She did. But as the day crept by, the more excited she got for the party and the less tired she felt. Funny how that worked.

She made a quick stop at her apartment to change, opting for comfy pink leggings and an oversized tunic sweater that had a big red heart on the front instead of her formal work clothes. It was a party for Littles, after all, and she loved that she could go over there and be her most authentic self. None of the men in the club ever made her feel weird or awkward. They all seemed to love having Littles around and being in their own caregiver headspaces.

After tossing her uncomfortable heels into the right side of her closet, she shifted the doors to look in the left side. She kept her big-girl clothes separated so she didn't even have to look at them when she was at home.

Hmm. Converse. Vans. Slippers. Ballet flats. Mary Janes.

She tapped her chin, trying to decide. It was hard to make the choice. That was something Brook was terrible at. When she'd stared at the shoes for too long, she rolled her eyes at herself.

"Stupid, just choose some shoes," she murmured to herself.

Bending down, she grabbed the slip-on white Vans. Good enough.

Once she was satisfied with her outfit, Brook went into the bathroom and pulled the claw clip from her long chestnut-brown hair, letting it fall free. The relief was instantaneous. With each step, it was like she was shedding her adult personality. Every time she did this, it was so freeing. Responsibilities sucked.

She took a few minutes to style her hair into a set of big fat space buns on the top of her head, letting a few loose whisps frame her face. One glance at her phone and she scurried back into her room to grab her small backpack purse and the gift she'd bought for Carlee. If she didn't hurry, she would be late.

Luckily, the Shadowridge Guardians' compound wasn't too far from her apartment, though it was in a more industrial part of the small town. Part of the compound housed a business that repaired motorcycles along with some other stuff the guys did. The front gate was already open so she pulled in and drove to the parking spaces behind the shop, where the actual clubhouse was.

A few men were outside talking, and as she got out of her car, she swallowed nervously. They were big and tattooed, and quite frankly, they were terrifying. She thought she'd seen them before when she'd been there but couldn't remember for sure.

As soon as the men saw her, they smiled and waved.

"Brook," the older man called out. "Good to see you again, Little one. The girls are all inside."

She gave the man a weak smile, feeling awful that he remembered her name, but she had no clue what his was.

He must have understood because he chuckled. "I'm Rock. And this is King and Faust."

Right. She had met them all before. Whoops.

"Sorry," she said as she fingered the strap of her backpack. "There's just so many of you."

King winked at her. "No worries, love. We all look similar, too. Though, I'm the handsomest one, obviously."

Faust snorted and shook his head. "Jesus Christ. Don't fucking scare the girl off."

She looked between the men, unsure what to say or do. A shudder worked its way through her. Faust was... well, he was one scary dude. Always had a scowl on his face. She remembered that from the first time she'd met him. Was his face just like that, or was he as mean as he looked?

Feeling bad for thinking that, she looked up at Faust and forced a kind smile. His face twitched like he was trying to smile back, but it looked more like a scowl.

Right. Time to move along.

"Nice seeing you guys again," she said as she headed toward the clubhouse entrance.

"You too, Brook. We'll be in there in a bit," Rock replied.

She liked Rock. The man was older and looked tough, but he had some sort of reassuring fatherly vibe about him that made her feel super safe.

As soon as she opened the door, she was met with squeals and screams of excitement. Atlas, Carlee's Daddy, noticed her first. He rose from his seat at a table surrounded by a bunch of other bikers. There was something about being in a room full of muscular, tattooed, slightly unkept men that made Brook tingle between her thighs. The men felt a little dangerous, but she wasn't afraid of them.

"Hey, Brook." Atlas strode toward her, calling out at the same time, "Carlee, Brook is here."

Carlee hooted and came running into the common room.

"No running!" at least five of the men barked.

Brook rolled her lips in to keep from grinning. The way the guys fussed over the women was adorable. Sometimes when she left the clubhouse, Brook would have a longing for a Daddy to worry about her. If she were totally honest with herself, the longing was always there, just under the surface of her independent self. It would never happen for her, though. Brook wasn't the type of girl guys wanted to get into a relationship with. And that was okay.

"I'm so glad you could come!" Carlee jumped up and down, clapping her hands together.

Her friend's excitement was so contagious that Brook started wiggling with her own excitement as she started to slip into her smaller headspace. It was so easy to do it here.

Other women ran into the room, also getting barked at by several men to slow down. Brook recognized Ivy, Remi, Harper, Eden, Elizabeth, and Addie, but she didn't recognize the last woman.

"This is Molly! Faust is her Daddy," Carlee introduced.

Brook started choking slightly. The huge scary dude was this sweet-looking woman's Daddy? Wow.

"Sorry." She coughed. "Air went down the wrong pipe, I guess."

Remi scrunched her nose. "Hate it when that happens."

They all nodded, giggling together.

"We were playing a game in the playroom. Wanna join?" Carlee asked, already tugging Brook toward the room tucked just off the common area.

"Food will be ready in an hour," Gabriel called out.

Brook was pretty sure he was Eden's Daddy, but she was still trying to remember all the men and which Little they were with.

As the girls passed the large table with all the men, Brook's heart started to race as she met the dark eyes of the hottest man she'd ever seen. The same man she'd fantasized about the night before.

*Storm.*

Time seemed to stand still as they locked gazes, both of their heads turning to keep contact as Brook walked by. It wasn't until the women entered the playroom that she lost view of those piercing, nearly black eyes.

She blinked a few times and then looked at her friends, who seemed to be grinning… at her.

"Did you just have an orgasm? Because that was totally an orgasmic stare-off," Carlee said, waggling her eyebrows at Brook.

"What?" Brook scoffed, waving her off. "You're silly."

Carlee rolled her eyes. "Okay. Whatever you say, even though I totally saw what I saw."

She *totally* did not see anything.

Licking her lips, she let out a breath. "He came into my office the other day to make an offer on a house. He was kind of a jerk."

Remi nibbled on one of her black-painted fingernails. *"That* would be Storm."

"Wait," Ivy said, drawing her eyebrows together. "Did you just say he's buying a house?"

# THREE
## STORM

S torm stared toward the playroom, sitting so still he was practically a statue. It was her. The one he wanted to scold yesterday for sleeping at her desk without locking the door. For staying up too late and not eating her lunch. He had suspected she could be Little, but there was no doubt about it now. The woman was fucking *Little*.

He hadn't caught her name when Carlee introduced Molly to her. They had been on the other side of the room, and he had been too stunned about seeing her again to think about going to introduce himself.

"You okay, bud?" Steele, the club president and Storm's best friend, asked.

Tearing his gaze away from the arched entrance to the room, Storm cleared his throat and nodded. "Fine. I should go."

It was usually what he did whenever the girls had a

party. He would head to his apartment for the night and watch a game or something.

As he rose from his seat, the swarm of girls stomped out of the playroom, hands on their hips. Except for the receptionist. She was standing behind them, her eyes shifting around nervously.

"You're moving?" Ivy demanded, shooting daggers his way.

The entire room fell silent. Fuck. He hadn't planned to tell everyone yet. Only a few select guys.

When he looked from Ivy to the adorable Little girl in the back, she mouthed, "*I'm so sorry.*"

Now he had another reason he wanted to scold her. More importantly, he wanted to know what else she had told the girls about him. He had a feeling when he'd left the real estate office the day before that she wasn't all that impressed by him. Most women weren't once he opened his mouth. He wasn't the smoothest guy.

"Why would you want to move? Do you not like us?" Remi asked in a small voice that clutched his heart tightly.

"What?" he snapped. "Why would you think that?"

Seriously, what was the big deal? A lot of the men in the club had homes of their own.

Remi rolled her eyes. Something she excelled at. "Gee, I don't know. Maybe because you're always grumpy to us, and now you're moving to get away from us." Remi sounded heartbroken.

"Remi," Kade said gently. "Don't make him feel bad. He's allowed to move if he wants to. He'll still have his apartment here."

Carlee sniffed, and Storm was pretty sure some water-works were about to start. He felt like such an asshole.

"Listen," he said, sharper than he meant, making a couple of the Littles startle. *Yeah, a total asshole.* "I'm not moving to get away from you. I'll still be at the compound nearly every day for work and club stuff, so you'll see me all the time."

"Why didn't you tell us? We could have had a meeting about it and voted for you to stay," Eden told him, tears forming in her wide eyes.

The fact that these Littles were so upset about him leaving was surprising to him. He wasn't quite sure how to feel about that. If anything, he thought they would have been happy to get rid of him.

Letting out a sigh, he ran a hand through his black slicked-back hair. Dealing with emotional shit wasn't his thing. He wasn't good at being vulnerable. The one time he'd let himself get attached, it had blown up in his face. It was better to keep messy things, like feelings, locked deep in the shell of his black heart.

"It's not like I'm moving far. I just made the offer yesterday. I was going to wait to see if it's accepted before I told everyone," he explained.

"Girls," Gabriel said. "Let's not worry about this tonight. You're all supposed to be having fun."

Remi huffed and crossed her arms over her chest. "Fine. But this conversation isn't over."

And then, just like they stormed in, the Littles disappeared back to the playroom as dramatically.

He leaned back in his chair and dropped his head to look at the ceiling. "I don't know why they're upset."

Steele stood, shaking his head. "Because whether you believe it or not, they love you, even though you're a cranky asshole."

"Fuck," Storm muttered. "How can I fix this?"

Gabriel smirked. "You could start by staying for the entire party."

Shit.

There went his plans.

At least there was one positive to staying.

He'd get to stare at the sweet ray of sunshine for the rest of the evening.

During the next hour, Storm couldn't stop himself from glancing toward the playroom every so often. He wasn't normally a curious person, but when he'd walked into the real estate office the day before, the receptionist had piqued his interest. She'd said she was tired because she'd stayed up late. Why was she up late, though? And why did he care or want to know? It didn't matter what her reasons were. He didn't know her; her life was none of his business.

So why did he have an urge to *make* it his business?

"Dinner's ready," Gabriel told the men.

Kade stood and crossed the room. "I'll tell the girls to go wash their hands."

As Gabriel brought several large dishes to the dining table, Faust set out plates for everyone while Doc filled sippy cups of watered-down juice for the girls. Smart guy. The last thing they needed was the Littles to get even more hopped-up on sugar. Storm was convinced they had a bag of candy hidden somewhere and had been eating it all afternoon. Not to mention the cake they would be eating later. He almost felt sorry for his club brothers who would have to deal with their Little girls at the end of the night when they had sugar crashes and became overly tired and unreasonable.

He continued to watch as his closest friends all working together to make sure everything was set up for dinner. It was their nightly routine. Storm had a tightness in his chest and something that felt like longing in the pit of his stomach. What would it be like to take care of someone again? Someone to protect and provide for. It's been so long since he had that. He couldn't really remember what it had been like.

One by one, the girls filed in with Kade trailing them, laughing at something Remi had said. The corners of Storm's lips twitched as he watched the couple while Kade helped his girl into a chair and then pushed her in.

"Hey. I want to apologize."

Turning toward the sweet voice, Storm met the eyes of the Little girl who ratted him out to everyone. "No need."

She let out a deep breath and nodded, though she kept rubbing her fingers over her fuzzy sweater as if the softness was soothing her. "I didn't realize they didn't know. I guess I assumed, and I shouldn't have. Anyway, I'm really sorry. I understand if you want to complain to my boss. I'm also sorry they got upset with you."

Unable to let her continue, Storm reached out to wrap

his hand around her dainty wrist and gently rub his thumb over her pulse point. "Look at me," he commanded as gently as he could, which wasn't great, but he couldn't help it. "You don't need to apologize. It was an accident. I should have told them, so it's on me, okay? I don't want you feeling bad about it."

Her shoulders dropped, and he hated that she'd been so stressed about it. He could be a jerk, but he wasn't a total asshole. Not usually, anyway.

"Okay," she murmured, lowering her eyes from his. "Thank you."

His heart raced. She was about to move away from him. Even if it was across the table, it was too far. Instead of letting her go, with his free hand, he pulled out the chair beside him. "Sit right here, Little girl."

She looked at the open seat and then around the room where her friends were spread out around the table. He hated that she was hesitating, but she was sitting next to him whether she liked it or not. He would get a booster chair and strap her in if he had to.

Fuck. What was wrong with him?

When she finally sat on the chair, he nodded and pushed her in.

"What's your name, sunshine?" he asked. "I didn't catch it before."

There was a pause before she tilted her head back and met his gaze. "Brook."

Brook. That was cute. Just like her.

In the short amount of time he'd seen her here at the clubhouse, he'd noticed several things about her. The first was that she was much quieter than the other girls. Maybe because she was a guest, but he thought it might actually be how she was all the time. She was quiet and reserved in the real estate office as well. The other thing he'd noticed was that she looked even more tired than the day before. It bothered him that she wasn't getting enough sleep.

"I'm Storm," he replied.

Slowly, her lips curled up into a smile. "I know. I worked on your file yesterday."

Right. Way to make her think he was a dumbass.

"Brook, do you want a hamburger, a piece of chicken, or a hot dog?" Atlas called from the end of the table.

Storm's stomach clenched. He glared at his friend, barely biting his tongue from snapping that he would help Brook get dished up. Why did it matter if Atlas was helping her?

Atlas noticed the death stare from Storm and returned it with a smug smile.

"Um, chicken? Well, actually, maybe a hamburger. Those hot dogs look good, too." She ducked her head, her cheeks turning bright red. "Sorry. I'm terribly indecisive. Chicken is fine."

"Nothing wrong with being indecisive, sunshine," Storm told her as he reached over and picked up her plate. "There's also nothing wrong with having a little of everything."

Then he looked pointedly at Atlas and raised a brow. "I got this."

Carlee whispered something to Ivy, who leaned over and repeated whatever it was into Remi's ear. When he shot them a stern look, the three of them smiled innocently.

Why did he get the feeling the topic of their whispering was him?

When he had Brook's plate filled with a bit of each dish, he set it in front of her. "Try a bite of everything, and if there's something you don't like, you don't have to eat it."

Brook stared up at him, her mouth open slightly. "Thank you. I could have gotten my own meal."

Shaking his head, he reached for a hamburger for himself and then took the other half of the one he cut from hers. "Little girls don't get their own food here. We have to make sure it's not too hot and that it's cut up so you don't choke."

As Storm tore into his dinner with hearty, voracious bites, Brook delicately nibbled at hers, savoring each small morsel with an elegance that seemed almost unconscious. While he devoured his plate in minutes, her meal remained mostly untouched, her fork hovering hesitantly as though she were lost in thought.

The room hummed with energy, the low rumble of deep voices mingling with the bubbly chatter and peals of laughter from the Littles. Despite the chaos, Storm felt an unexpected sense of satisfaction seeing how effortlessly everyone included Brook, treating her as though she'd always been a part of their close-knit clubhouse family. But his sharp eyes didn't miss the moments when she quieted, her bright green eyes darting around the room, observing on the periphery rather than engaging. She didn't seem uncomfortable, exactly—just quiet, soaking in her surroundings. Something Storm understood completely.

Every so often, out of the corner of his eye, he'd catch

her peeking over at him. What was she thinking? Was she scared of him? He knew he was intimidating, even when he was trying not to be. Did she think he was attractive? He certainly found her to be beautiful.

Those shining green eyes of hers and her pillowy lips made it hard not to stare at her. Add in her wide hips and big tits and he was practically drooling. He shouldn't assume she was single, but fuck, if she were his, she wouldn't go anywhere without him. If she did have a man, Storm already hated the guy. She was too damn precious to be out and about on her own.

"I've never seen you here when I've come over before," she said quietly.

Leaning back, he turned so his body was slightly angled toward her. For some reason, he wanted to give her his full attention. "I don't socialize a lot. I like to keep to myself."

Great. That wasn't the right thing to say if he wanted her to like him. His words hung in the air like an awkward pause, and he inwardly cringed. He might as well have slapped a neon sign across his chest that read, *I'm a grumpy recluse—proceed with caution.* The mental image of himself standing there, arms crossed, and a scowl etched into his face, was enough to make him grimace. Perfect. Just the impression he wanted to leave. *Smooth, Storm. Real smooth.*

Brook held his gaze for a lingering moment, her emerald-green eyes shimmering with empathy, a soft smile curling at the corners of her pillowy lips. "I understand." Her voice was a gentle melody that threaded between the hum of conversation around them. "I'm the same way, actually. I'm so introverted. I love coming to hang out with the girls, but afterward…" She paused, her smile deepening, a faint blush warming her cheeks. "I'm going to have to hibernate in my apartment for the rest of the weekend to recharge." Her tone held a self-deprecating warmth, the kind of honesty that felt both vulnerable and endearing.

Ah. Now her quiet observing made sense.

Her eyes went wide, and she covered her mouth. "Sorry. That was probably TMI."

For the first time in a long time, he chuckled. She was too fucking cute. "Not TMI, sunshine. Is that why you were so tired yesterday?"

Her cheeks turned bright pink again. Storm's gaze lingered, captivated by the innocent beauty of her reaction. Would she blush like that in bed? The thought struck him hard, unbidden and intoxicating. He imagined those same cheeks glowing for an entirely different reason, her wide, green eyes alight with unrestrained passion. Sweet, so fucking sweet, and innocent, like temptation wrapped in an adorable little package. The vivid image sent a surge of heat through him, and his body responded instantly, tension coiling low in his belly. His cock ached, and he had to shift to make it more comfortable to sit.

"No, I was up reading late the night before. It's sort of a bad habit of mine. I get lost in a book and can't put it down until I can't keep my eyes open any longer."

He didn't like that. Not one bit. How many hours of sleep was she getting each night? Not enough, based on the dark circles under her eyes that her concealer didn't fully cover.

"Brook, do you want to come play a game with us?" Carlee called out.

Storm had to bite back a growl. He wasn't done talking to Brook. For the first time in a very long time, he wanted to have a conversation with someone. She was here for the party, though, not for him, and he wouldn't take away her chance to play with her friends.

"Coming!" Brook stood and then picked up her plate, but Storm stopped her and took it from her hands.

She was a tiny little thing compared to him. She had to tilt her head way back to look at him. And fuck if that didn't turn him on.

"Go play. I'll take care of this," he said.

After a second of staring at him, she flashed him an adorable grin before she turned and skipped toward her friends.

"Be good," he warned without thinking better of it.

When the girls were out of sight, he let out a breath and turned toward the kitchen. He froze, though, because all his brothers were grinning at him like they knew something he didn't.

"What?" he demanded.

Kade looked toward Steele. "Are you going to tell him?"

Steele chuckled and shook his head. "Nah. We'll wait for him to figure it out on his own. Just like we had to."

Confused and annoyed, especially because he couldn't see Brook any longer, Storm flipped them off and then stomped to the kitchen while his so-called friends burst into laughter.

And they called *him* an asshole.

# FOUR
## BROOK

Brook couldn't stop thinking about Storm. His scent lingered in her mind, clean yet rugged, with a hint of leather and something uniquely him—something that made her head swim every time she caught a whiff of it. Then there were his eyes, dark as midnight, almost black, yet smoldering with an intensity that pierced right through her. The way he had looked at her with those eyes, a mix of curiosity, danger, and something deeper, had left her breathless, as though he could see deep into her soul. She didn't want to admit it—not even to herself—but she was just as curious about him. There was a quiet magnetism between them, an allure that tugged at her thoughts, no matter how hard she tried to push them away.

It was entirely possible he wasn't single. Just because his woman wasn't there didn't mean he was without one. Although, if he did have someone in his life, Brook felt sorry for them because she was pretty sure he'd been flirting with her all night. Even Daddying her slightly with how he had prepared her plate of food. She'd started sweating a bit when Atlas asked her what she wanted to eat. In the moment, she felt stupid for not being able to make a choice. It was embarrassing. But Storm stepped in and took care of things. He helped in a way that wasn't what she'd expected from him.

After she'd accidentally spilled the beans about him buying a house, Brook had been sure he would yell at her. Or, at the very least, tell her boss. Instead, he'd met her apology with gentle words and forgiveness. Storm might be a bit grumpy, but she was pretty sure there was something a little more gentle underneath his exterior.

"I can't wait for cake!" Carlee squealed, wiggling in her spot on the floor as they played Barbies. "I asked Bear for an Oreo cake with extra frosting."

Now that was something Brook could get on board with. Extra frosting. Her pudgy tummy and jiggly thighs didn't need it, but her heart did, and that was the most important organ. Yep. She'd go with that.

Brook dug through a box of Barbie shoes, looking for the match to a stiletto that no one in real life could ever actually wear. "Wow, a man in the clubhouse who bakes? And an amazing cook? Gabriel's dinner was delicious. Even the carrots and they're not usually my favorite."

Carlee giggled. "They've started figuring out ways to make vegetables taste delicious because they got tired of us not eating them."

That was sweet of their Daddies.

"What did you and Storm talk about at dinner?" Ivy asked.

Brook shrugged. "Nothing, really. I was nervous and ended up blabbing about being an introvert. He probably thinks I'm weird."

Eden snorted. "With the way he kept his eyes on you the entire time, I'd say he was too busy falling in love to think anything bad about you."

She burst out laughing at Eden because that was just ridiculous! She'd just met the man. Until dinner, he hadn't known her name.

"You might need to get your vision checked because he wasn't looking at me like *that*," Brook replied.

What she didn't say was that there was no way in hell a man like Storm would ever be interested in a woman like her.

Molly nibbled on her bottom lip, looking around nervously. "I don't know. I kind of agree with Eden. Storm definitely seemed different at dinner. Quieter. Softer. Not the same brooding, hard-edged guy we're so used to seeing around here." Her tone carried a mix of disbelief and wonder, as if the change in Storm's demeanor was as fascinating as it was unsettling.

Brook frowned. "Is he usually mean?"

She didn't like the idea of that. If he treated her friends badly, she'd… well, she'd do something about it. Probably not herself, but she wouldn't hesitate to tell one of their Daddies because she could tell none of those men would allow anyone to be mean to their Little girls, even someone in the club.

Harper shook her head. "No. None of the men here are ever mean to us. Storm is just… grumpy. Like when you think of The Grinch, Storm is like him but times ten. But he's nice and does kind things for us sometimes."

Hmm. Why was he so grumpy? The question tugged at the edges of her thoughts, persistent and curious. Had something in his past shaped him into the brooding, closed-off man he appeared to be? Or had he always been that way, carrying an air of restless intensity like a second skin? Had he always been someone who didn't' enjoy being around lots of noise? She didn't know why she cared. It wasn't her place to wonder, and it was certainly none of her business. Storm was just a stranger, someone who had momentarily crossed her path. After tonight, their lives would drift apart like ships passing in the dark.

And yet, the thought of never seeing him again left an unexpected pang in her chest, a dull ache she couldn't quite explain. It was ridiculous—completely irrational— but the idea of his dark eyes and gruff voice becoming nothing more than a memory felt... wrong. She shook her head, trying to dismiss the melancholy settling over her, but the sadness lingered, quiet and stubborn, like a question she couldn't find the answer to.

"Happy birthday to youuuuu!" everyone finished singing.

Carlee beamed, and Brook was pretty sure if she grinned any wider her face would split in two. It was sweet. She loved seeing her friend so happy and loved.

As soon as Carlee blew out the candles, Atlas pulled

them from the frosting. He dropped them onto a small paper cake plate and then scanned the table. "Shit, I forgot a knife. I'll be right back."

Remi reached over to put her finger in a corner of the frosting where no one would notice, and at the same time, it was almost as if a light bulb lit up over Carlee's head.

She sat up straight and tipped her head, a smirk on her lips. "That's okay, Daddy. We don't need a knife. We can feed each other."

Without a moment's hesitation, Carlee plunged her fingers right into the center of the cake. The vibrant icing squished between her fingers, and with a mischievous grin, she swiped it across Remi's cheek in one bold, sticky streak. Remi froze for a split second, her eyes wide with shock before a squeal erupted from her lips, high-pitched and full of disbelief.

But the surprise didn't last long. With a quick, retaliatory maneuver, Remi scooped up a handful of frosting and smeared it across Carlee's face, her movements swift and unrelenting. Carlee let out a giggle that turned into a full-blown laugh, the sound bubbling over as the sugary chaos began to unfold.

Before Brook could fully process what was happening, frosting and cake chunks were flying through the air. Ivy took aim, walloping a dollop of frosting across Brook's cheek with an unapologetic grin. Brook retaliated instantly, smooshing a handful of sticky sweetness onto Ivy's face, her laughter mingling with the squeals and shrieks echoing through the room.

The chaos grew louder, more joyful, as frosting-covered fingers and excitement filled the air. The girls moved with reckless abandon, their screams of delight punctuated by giggles that turned into uncontrollable laughter. Frosting clung to faces, hair, and clothes, the once-perfect cake now a battlefield of sugary mayhem. It was wild, messy, and absolutely everything—a moment of unrestrained joy none of them would soon forget.

It was chaos.

Pure and innocent. But total chaos.

"Freeze!" Steele boomed, cutting through the noise.

Each Little froze in place, including Brook. She glanced around, taking in the mess they'd created, which was a bit horrifying. It looked like the cake had exploded.

"Did you girls not learn anything from the last birthday party?" Steele demanded, his eyes narrowed.

Yikes. Steele was intimidating when he was like this.

Remi put her index finger in her mouth and sucked off the frosting, pulling it out with a loud pop. "Well, I don't know about the rest of the girls, but I learned I like Oreo cake more than chocolate cake."

"Remi!" Kade scolded. "Watch the sass. You're already in enough trouble."

Trouble? Oh, shoot. Brook hadn't thought about that. Were the men *really* mad?

As she slowly scanned each of their stern faces, it seemed like a few were struggling to keep from laughing.

"Daddy, it's a tradition. We have to smear cake on each other at our birthdays. Picture it like mud wrestling, but instead, we use delicious frosting," Carlee said, grinning up at Atlas.

Out of the corner of her eye, someone shifted, catching her attention. When she turned, her gaze collided with

Storm's. He stared back at her, his expression every bit as stern as it had been earlier, his dark eyes locked onto hers with an intensity that sent a shiver down her spine. Unlike the other men, there was no trace of a smile tugging at the corners of his mouth. His gaze was steady, unyielding, and wholly unreadable.

*Uh oh.*

Brook swallowed hard, her heart skipping a beat as her cheeks heated. She couldn't look away, even though every instinct told her she should. Her pulse quickened when she noticed the subtle movement of his hand. His fingers brushed over his short beard, slow and deliberate, but she didn't miss the way his hand seemed to twitch once, twice, and then a third, as though resisting the urge to act.

At that moment, she was deeply relieved Storm *wasn't* her Daddy because if he had been, she had no doubt she'd be in trouble.

"You naughty girls are cleaning up this mess. And tonight, before bed, I'm sure we'll all be having a chat."

Brook was pretty sure a chat meant a spanking. Carlee told her that Atlas spanked her *a lot*, but only because she wanted and needed it. Most of the time she was naughty, it was on purpose just so she would end up over his knee.

She peeked at Storm's hand again and squeezed her thighs together. What would it be like to be spanked by the man? His hand was in proportion to the rest of him. He was so big and broad, even with her curves, she was sure he could hold her down.

Crap. That thought sent a tingle through her, right down to her pussy. Her breasts suddenly felt heavier and more sensitive, and her heart raced. When was the last time she'd gotten turned on by thoughts of a man? She had no idea, but even then, she'd never reacted to anyone this intensely.

"Sorry, Daddy," Carlee said softly.

Atlas smirked. "You're forgiven, baby. It's not like we're really surprised. You girls truly seem determined to make this a tradition no matter how hard we paddle your butts when you do it."

Heat radiated from Brook's core, and she dipped her head, unable to keep her gaze on Storm. Despite that, she felt his stare practically searing into her.

"Okay, get this cleaned up. I suggest you don't start a second food fight while you do," Kade told them.

Several of the men provided them with cleaning supplies and then left Brook and the other Littles to wipe up the mess. It really was a waste of good cake, but dang, it was also a blast.

By the time the whirlwind of the evening finally settled and all traces of the frosting explosion had been cleaned up, Brook was utterly exhausted, her body heavy with a pleasant fatigue. Yet, despite her tired limbs and the slight ache in her cheeks from hours of laughter and smiles, she felt a sense of overwhelming joy. A glow of contentment warmed her from the inside out, the kind of happiness that only came from feeling truly connected.

When she'd first met Carlee at the library, Brook had been thrilled to find someone who shared her passion for books. Carlee's infectious enthusiasm and easy friendship had been a gift. But now, after spending hours with the group of women—sharing stories, laughter, and even a ridiculous, frosting-laden cake fight—Brook felt something deeper. These weren't just acquaintances or casual companions anymore. They felt like her tribe, a circle of genuine friends who had welcomed her with open arms.

Her heart swelled with gratitude, the realization sinking in that she didn't just have a friend in Carlee; she had a whole gaggle of women who were her chosen family. And for someone who'd always been a little reserved, a little cautious about letting people in, that was everything.

Around ten, when she could barely keep her eyes open any longer while they watched a movie, Brook sighed and forced herself up from the comfy beanbag seat she'd curled up on.

"I should probably go," she told Carlee, who was also fighting to stay awake.

"You can stay the night if you want," Carlee offered as she stood.

Brook hugged her friend and shook her head. "Thank you. I don't sleep very well without Bubbles."

Her friend nodded. "I understand. I need at least one of my stuffies otherwise, I won't get a wink."

After hugging all the other women who were still awake, Brook grabbed her backpack and smiled when Atlas appeared and explained that he would walk her to her car.

It seemed all these men were overprotective.

And she definitely didn't hate it.

Storm was outside the clubhouse near her car, talking to another club member. She slowed her steps and kept an eye on him as she approached.

"Night, Brook. Drive home safe," Atlas said before he retreated inside.

The man who had been talking to Storm suddenly seemed to disappear, leaving her alone in the night with the man who did strange things to her insides.

"I'm following you home," he informed her matter-of-factly as he grabbed a helmet off the handlebar of a motorcycle.

Was that his bike? Wow. Black and sleek. She'd never ridden and wasn't sure she would like it, but picturing Storm riding was a sexy thought.

"Oh, you don't need to do that."

He arched a brow, his face stern. "I didn't ask, sunshine. It's late, dark, and the roads are wet from the rain earlier. I'm following you. Don't forget to wear your seatbelt."

It didn't take a genius to see that he wasn't going to back down.

She let out a dramatic sigh and opened her door. "Fine. But this is totally unnecessary."

And a total turn-on.

She would keep that part to herself.

She kept glancing in her rearview mirror even though she really didn't need to. The low growl of his motorcycle reminded her that he was still there during the entire drive home.

Letting out a sigh, she tightened her hands around the steering wheel. She didn't need an escort. She'd driven home by herself lots of times in the dark, in the rain, and late at night. And as much as she had wanted to argue that point with him, she was also kind of touched that he took it upon himself to make sure she was safe.

As soon as she parked and stepped out of her car, Storm pulled his bike up behind her and cut the engine.

"You really didn't need to follow me," she told him again.

His face was unreadable. It made her shift nervously, unsure if she should say something else or just turn around and walk inside.

"Did you have fun tonight?" he asked.

Surprised by his question, she blinked several times. Why did he care if she had?

"Yes, thank you. I did." She smiled as she thought about it.

"Yeah? You were quite naughty getting into that cake fight." His tone was light but still held an edge. Her bottom clenched at the word *naughty*.

"I didn't start it." Yeah, that was a good argument.

Storm smirked and shook his head. "You still participated, sunshine."

Her mouth fell open. He kept calling her that, and it was starting to feel special. She hadn't heard him use that nickname with the other girls. Was it just for her?

When she didn't respond immediately, his low chuckle rumbled through the air, deep and smooth like distant thunder. "Wash your face and brush your teeth, then go to bed. No reading tonight. You need sleep. Got me?"

Her mind stalled. *Huh?*

Was he... telling her what to do? As if he were her Daddy?

The audacity sent a jolt through her, though she couldn't deny the logic in his words. She was utterly drained, close to falling asleep, but still... He wasn't the boss of her. Nope. She was in charge of herself, thank you very much—well, mostly. Even if her recent choices hadn't exactly been stellar examples of self-care.

Her pulse quickened, confusion tangling with a flicker of irritation that coiled inside her tummy. Was she really about to challenge him? The idea was as startling as it was exhilarating, her exhaustion lending her a bravery she wasn't sure she possessed.

"Since when do *you* get to tell *me* what to do?" she shot back, her voice steady despite the wild fluttering in her chest.

Wow. Where had *that* come from?

Storm's dark eyes locked onto hers, the weight of his gaze making her feel exposed *and* electrified. His lips curved slightly, the ghost of a smile teasing at the edges of his mouth. Was he... amused?

"Since right now, sunshine," he replied, his tone quiet but firm, carrying an authority that made the night air hum with unspoken tension. He leaned in slightly, the intensity in his gaze somehow softening without losing its intensity. "You were barely able to stay awake during the movie, and you admitted to staying up late for the past couple of nights. Someone has to look out for you."

The space between them seemed to crackle, the charged silence stretching as his words settled over her. There was no malice in his voice, no mocking—just a steady, unyielding care that was as disarming as it was infuriating.

"So, yeah, I'm telling you what to do, and you're going to be a good girl and do it, aren't you?"

She crossed her arms defensively, suddenly feeling very Little. It wasn't just that he was right. It was how he said it, as if he was her Daddy.

"You don't get to—"

"I get to do whatever I want, sunshine," he interrupted, unwavering, like it was a fact.

Her breath caught, a flash of something soft and vulnerable rising in her chest.

"You're not my boss," she muttered, taking a step back.

He chuckled again, the sound warm but with an edge of something else, something teasing. "Nah. But I am the one who told you to go wash your face. And guess what? You're going to do it."

She stiffened, a blush creeping up her neck despite herself. Damn him.

"Fine," she huffed, turning to go up the walkway and trying her best to act unaffected, though her heart was still hammering against her ribcage.

When she reached the front door and pulled out her key to unlock it, she took one more peek back at him.

"Goodnight, sunshine," he called out, almost gently.

"Goodnight, Storm."

And when she got inside and changed into her pajamas —after washing her face, of course—ignoring her e-reader completely, she couldn't shake the warm feeling inside her tummy. She didn't know Storm, but she was pretty sure she wanted that to change.

# FIVE
## STORM

Storm leaned back in one of the old leather chairs in the common room. He was pretty sure the thing had been around since the club had formed. They really needed to upgrade some of the furniture. Something that ancient couldn't be safe for the Littles.

He absently peeled the label from his beer bottle. The third one he'd had since he got back from following Brook home. Across the room, Steele reclined on one of the couches, Ivy sound asleep in his lap.

"So," Steele began softly, dragging out the word as though testing the waters of a conversation he wasn't entirely sure he wanted to have. His voice was calm but probing, like a fisherman casting a line and waiting to see if it would snag. "You gonna tell me why you're making confetti out of your beer labels, or should I guess?"

Storm shot him a dry look, but the irritation didn't last long. It crumbled under the weight of his own frustration, and he sighed heavily, his shoulders slumping. He set the half-empty beer bottle down with more force than intended, the glass clinking sharply against the table. Ivy stirred in Steele's lap, prompting the club president to glare at Storm in silent reprimand.

"Sorry," Storm muttered, his words came out low, rough with something he didn't want to name. He hesitated for a beat, his fingers brushing over the pile of shredded beer labels like he could smooth away his turmoil. Finally, he admitted, "It's Brook."

Steele's grin spread slowly, smug and knowing. "Pretty much already figured that out, genius. I've known you all our lives." He leaned back, letting out a quiet half laugh. "You like her. Haven't seen you look at someone like that since…"

His friend's words hung in the air, heavy with history, and for once, Storm was grateful his friend let them trail off. He didn't need *her* name spoken aloud, didn't need the weight of that memory crashing into the room, sullying the atmosphere. It had no place here.

"It's not a thing," Storm muttered, his tone defensive, almost desperate to dismiss the thoughts tangling in his head. He dragged a hand through his dark hair, sighing. "She's… I don't know, man. Brook's cute. Sweet. The kind of person who smiles at everyone, you know? A little ray of fucking sunshine."

Steele nodded, though the smirk never left his face. "Yeah," he said, his tone dripping with sarcasm, "the kind of sunshine that's dangerous. Definitely don't want anyone sweet or cute in your life, Storm. Might make you feel human for once. Can't have that, right?" Steele winked at Storm, knowing full-well what his words were doing.

Storm glared at him, and Steele's chuckle only deepened. The tension lingered as Storm reached for his beer again, his fingers tightening around the bottle.

"I'm serious," Storm whispered. His friends could be such assholes sometimes. "She's... different. Feels like she's got this light around her or something. Watching her in Little Space was addictive. It would never work out, but fuck, I had thoughts while she was here tonight."

"You're getting poetic on me now. This is worse than I thought. You're fucking sprung."

Storm scoffed and shook his head. "See, this is why I don't talk to you about this kind of stuff."

"Relax, I'm kidding." Steele beamed. "So, what's the problem? She's cute, you like her, she's Little, she's apparently glowing or something—sounds like a win to me."

"I don't know if I'd be... good for her," he admitted quietly. "She's got this positivity, this... I don't know, lightness. And I'm—" He gestured to himself, "Whatever this is. Dark. Broken. Fucking poison."

"You mean 'a grumpy loner with a good heart buried somewhere under all that pissed-off charm'?" Steele offered helpfully.

"Fuck off," Storm said dryly. "I don't want to drag her into my crap. I have trust issues. No one wants to deal with that bullshit. I know I'm an asshole."

"Look," Steele said as he flexed his feet in his reclined position, his tone measured but firm. "I get it. You're scared. Last time sucked—I know that better than anyone. But Brook's not Emmaline."

Storm flinched, the name hitting him like a slap, sharp and unwanted. It wasn't just the sound of it; it was the memories that came with the name. He hated even thinking about her.

Steele continued, "You didn't do anything wrong with Emmaline. She's the one who decided to go fuck ten other guys around town. Did she think you wouldn't find out? She was a terrible fucking person, Storm. Plain and simple. And yeah, I don't know Brook all that well yet, but I can already tell she's not like that. Not even close."

Storm stayed silent for a long moment, his jaw so tight it was painful. Finally, he sighed, his lips curving into a faint smirk that didn't quite reach his eyes. "You're annoyingly good at this pep-talk thing, you know that? You've gotten all wise and shit since you took over the club and found your Little girl."

"Perks of being your best friend," Steele shot back, the smile returning to his face, but this time, it carried a warmth that only years of camaraderie could forge. "Now it's your turn to become wise, dipshit. Take a chance."

Maybe Steele had a point. Maybe the past didn't have to dictate the future. Maybe, just maybe, Brook wasn't a risk but an opportunity.

Storm stood outside the real estate office, hesitating. It had been two days since he'd seen Brook, and he couldn't stay away any longer. He needed to set his eyes on her. To know if she'd slept. If she'd eaten. To make sure she wasn't skipping lunch or napping with the door unlocked again.

The faint hum of lunchtime traffic drifted through the air, mingling with the drool-worthy scent of fresh bread wafting from the bakery a few doors down. The crisp air filled his lungs as he took a steadying breath and then walked through the door.

Brook's gaze lifted from her computer screen, her bright eyes catching the sunlight streaming through the windows. The golden rays made them sparkle. Her face lit up with a genuine smile that warmed him down to his bones.

"Hi, Storm," she said a little unsteadily, as though surprised to see him.

"Hey, sunshine," he replied, low and casual, though his heart thudded harder than he liked to admit. "I was in the neighborhood and thought I'd see if you've had lunch yet."

"Not yet," she answered, her voice soft but intrigued.

"Good," was his firm yet surprisingly gentle response. "I came to take you to lunch. We can go to the diner."

Her cheeks flushed a delicate pink that matched the little bow she wore in her hair. The sight made his chest tighten. Damn, she was cute. Even dressed in her business clothes, she exuded the same sweet, playful energy he'd seen when she was in Little Space. It didn't matter what she wore; to him, she'd always be that endearing Little girl.

Brook swallowed, the movement drawing his attention to the graceful line of her neck. "You're asking me to lunch?"

"I don't usually ask, sunshine."

She blinked, her wide eyes studying him before she giggled softly. "I've kind of noticed." Her tone was playful.

She gestured to her computer. "Give me a minute to finish this email, and then we can go."

Storm nodded, leaning casually against the desk as he watched her type, her fingers moving swiftly over the keyboard. He couldn't stop himself from noticing the way her blush lingered. He loved it when she did that.

When they arrived at the diner, Storm slid into the booth across from her, wanting to see her face while they ate. The place was cozy—the typical 1950s style diner, with red vinyl seats and a jukebox in the corner.

He already knew what he wanted, but Brook seemed utterly engrossed in the menu, her gaze flicking across the pages. She reread it several times, her lips pressing together in concentration. Remembering her confession the other night, Storm reached across the table, tugging the menu from her hands.

"How many things are you trying to decide between?"

"Three," she admitted softly.

"What are they?"

"The cheeseburger, the Cobb salad, and the chicken strips."

Storm leaned back, watching her closely. He couldn't seem to tear his attention away from her even if he tried. "What did you have for dinner last night?"

"Um, chicken nuggets," she said, her voice barely above a whisper.

He arched an eyebrow, his expression both incredulous and teasing. "And?"

She lifted her gaze to meet his, the corners of her lips twitching like she was trying to hold back a smile. "And… ranch?"

He narrowed his eyes, leaning forward slightly as though to emphasize his point. "Is that a question, sunshine? Because if so, I don't have an answer for you. But if I'd been there, you damn sure would've had more than just chicken nuggets and ranch for dinner."

When she gave him a weak smile and didn't reply, he sighed heavily, shaking his head. "I'll order you the Cobb salad."

He noticed the subtle way her shoulders dropped, a flicker of disappointment passing over her features. He'd ignore it—for now. She'd understand soon enough.

After the waitress came by and he placed their order, the silence between them was slightly awkward. Brook fidgeted, her fingers brushing the edge of the table, while Storm stared at her, trying to decide what to say. Finally, he cleared his throat.

"I should tell you something," he began, his voice steady though his nerves prickled.

Brook raised her eyebrows. "Okay," she replied, drawing out the word.

He drew in a deep breath, the weight of what he had to say pressing against his chest. "I like you, Brook. A lot. Which is saying something because I don't fucking like anyone. I only met you at the end of last week, but ever since I first saw you in the real estate office, you've been on my mind."

Her mouth fell open slightly, looking surprised. How could she not know? She was stunning—those bright green eyes, that soft, pillowy smile—and she was so damn sweet it was fucking painful.

"Um, I don't know what to say," she finally managed

shakily as her gaze dropped to her lap before rising to meet his again.

He exhaled slowly, forcing himself to continue. "I'm not the easiest guy to be around," he admitted, his voice rough with honesty. "I can be... possessive. And trust doesn't come easy for me. I've been burned before."

Brook stayed quiet, her eyes studying him, her expression unreadable. When she finally spoke, she was calm, almost hesitant. "By a woman?"

"Yeah." He leaned forward, his eyes locking onto hers. "I just... if this goes anywhere, I want you to know what you're getting into."

The silence that followed was heavy but not uncomfortable, the magnitude of his confession settling between them as Brook processed his words.

Finally, she smiled, but it wasn't the dazzling grin that lit up the room and tugged at his chest. This one was smaller, softer, and tinged with a sadness that made his stomach twist. "Thank you for being honest," she said, a little quieter now... "And for what it's worth, I think you're a good guy, Storm. A little rough around the edges, maybe, but good."

Her gaze dropped to the table for a moment before she looked back up, her eyes filled with a hesitant vulnerability. "I'm an introvert, and I spend a lot of time reading or doing quiet things to decompress after work or hanging out with people. I pretty much hid in my bed all weekend after Friday night. The party was so much fun, but it takes me time to regroup after being social."

Storm's brow furrowed slightly. He didn't understand where she was going with this. Did she think he'd care?

Introvert or not, it didn't matter to him. He leaned back in his seat, crossing his arms as he waited for her to continue.

"What I'm trying to say," she added, her fingers fidgeting with the edge of her napkin, "is that I'm not great at relationships. I can't hold a conversation for hours, I don't like going out much, and honestly, watching movies or reading in bed is my idea of the perfect night."

Ah. Now he got it.

"Sunshine," he said, his voice steady and laced with dry amusement, "do I look fucking social to you?" He gestured to himself as though to drive the point home. "The only reason I stuck around for the whole party was because Steele guilt-tripped me about the house situation —and because *you* were there. Normally, I'd be in my apartment, hiding all night so I didn't have to deal with a bunch of people."

Brook blinked, her lips twitching as though she was fighting a smile. "Carlee was right. You do curse a lot."

That threw him off for a second, but then he chuckled gruffly. "Yeah, sunshine. I do."

Their conversation was interrupted as the waitress arrived, setting their plates on the table. Storm asked for an extra plate, and when it arrived, he immediately set to work. With deliberate movements, he cut his burger in half, added a generous handful of fries to the plate, and slid it across the table to her.

Brook tilted her head, her brows knitting together in confusion. "What's this for?"

"Give me some of your salad," he said. "We'll share. That way, you get to try two of the things you wanted, and I'll get my vegetables for the day."

She stared at him, her expression softening as a smile slowly playing across her face. "You're sharing your burger with me?"

He shrugged and took a massive bite of his half, chewing for a moment before swallowing. "Yeah, sunshine. And for the record, I don't share my food with just anyone."

Her grin widened, and for the first time since they sat down, he felt like he'd done something right.

Even though he could have downed three scoops of mint chocolate chip, by the time they left the diner, Brook turned down going for ice cream because of how full she was. It was cute the way she rubbed her tummy and groaned. Especially since she'd only had three bites of the burger, five fries, and a few bites of salad. Storm had polished off everything she hadn't.

"You're sure you don't want dessert?" he asked as they walked back toward the real estate office.

Giggling, she looked up at him. "I don't know where you put all that food."

"Between my hours in the shop and working out in the gym, I'm sure I burn most of it off. I've always eaten like that, though. My mom used to tell me I was going to eat them out of a home when I was a teenager."

Brook laughed, the sound floating through the air like a melody. His cock twitched, but he forced himself to ignore it, hoping it wouldn't embarrass him in the middle of Main Street.

When they stopped in front of her office, she turned to him, hesitated for a heartbeat, then stepped forward and wrapped her arms around his waist in a tight hug.

Storm froze for a second, his brain short-circuiting, but then his arms came up almost instinctively, holding her close. She smelled like soft powder and something sweet, and momentarily, everything felt startlingly perfect.

When she pulled back, she gave him that soft smile again. "Thanks for lunch."

He nodded, his throat suddenly dry. "Yeah. Anytime, sunshine."

As she slipped back inside, Storm stood there for a moment, staring after her. Something shifted inside him, something he hadn't felt in a long time. And it scared the hell out of him.

## SIX
# BROOK

All Brook wanted was to get home and strip away the weight of her adult headspace. The day had been long and challenging. While her job as a receptionist was usually pretty easy, today had been the complete opposite. Every so often, clients came along who were impossible to please, the type who expected the entire office to drop everything and show up at a property at a moment's notice. Unfortunately, today, they had *two* of those clients, and to make matters worse, both wanted the same house. It was a disaster waiting to happen, but thankfully, it wasn't her mess to clean up. The agents were the ones on the front line.

Still, the tension lingered, winding tight in her shoulders and causing her to have a headache as she drove through Shadowridge. She heaved a weary sigh, slowing as one of the town's rare traffic lights shifted from yellow to red. Her mind wandered, replaying the day's events, until the world jolted violently around her.

The loud crunch of metal filled her ears, sharp and shattering. Her head snapped forward, the seatbelt catching her just in time. For a moment, her vision blurred, her heart pounding so hard it felt like it might burst out of her chest. She stared at the red light ahead, unwavering in its glow, before dropping her gaze to her trembling hands white-knuckling the wheel.

She was fine. She repeated it in her mind like a mantra. Everything was fine. The airbags hadn't deployed. It wasn't anything major—just a fender bender. But even as she tried to convince herself of that, she quivered against the seat, her stomach churning with unease.

The sharp *slam* of a car door behind her snapped her out of the daze.

*Right. Get out. Make sure they're okay. Exchange information. No big deal.*

Moving took more energy than it should have. It felt like everything was going in slow motion. Her fingers fumbled with the seatbelt before she finally unbuckled it and pushed the driver's side door open. As she stepped out, she clung to the car's frame for balance, her legs unsteady beneath her. The cool air hit her flushed cheeks as she wobbled slightly, her ears ringing faintly from the impact. Nausea threatened as she tried to take some deep breaths.

A man stomped over from the red car behind her, his wrinkled polo straining against his round belly. As soon as he reached her, his hand shot out, jabbing a finger in her direction as his voice boomed through the stillness.

"You kidding me? You slammed your brakes out of nowhere!" he shouted so loud it made her jump.

Her pulse raced, and her stomach knotted tighter. She swallowed hard, struggling to find her voice. The adrenaline coursing through her veins made it hard to focus on anything other than the anger radiating from the red-faced man in front of her.

Brook blinked, trying to keep her tears at bay. It wasn't as though anyone had been seriously hurt, but it was her first car accident, and the shock of it was overwhelming.

"It was a red light," she explained, her voice trembling despite her best efforts to sound steady.

"Yeah, well, you stopped too fast!" he yelled, his voice echoing sharply as he threw his arms wide.

The man loomed over her, taller and wider, his flushed face glistening with sweat. His movements were erratic, his hands slicing through the air. Brook's stomach clenched tighter as he took a step closer, his voice rising.

"Do you have any idea how much this mess is gonna cost me?" he demanded. "You weren't even paying attention to what was around you!"

"I—" she tried to respond, but her throat closed up, the words catching before they could form. Her breath hitched, and the edges of her vision blurred as her ears filled with a faint ringing. A tear escaped, then another, tracing warm paths down her cheeks. Why was he so angry? Wasn't this why you got insurance?

And then, cutting through the noise like a lifeline, came a deep, familiar voice.

"Hey!"

Brook's head snapped toward the sound. Storm was climbing out of a sleek black truck parked on the curb, his dark eyes locked on the unfolding scene. The sight of him

—tall, broad, and commanding—was exactly what she needed to be able calm down enough to finally take a full breath.

He marched over with purpose, his long strides eating up the distance in seconds. His jaw was tight, and his gaze was fixed on the man like a hawk zeroing in on its prey. His sheer presence was enough to make the man falter, taking half a step back as Storm loomed closer.

"What's going on here?" Storm asked, his voice low and calm yet carrying an unmistakable edge of authority. He didn't shout, didn't need to. His tone alone demanded attention. His dark eyes swept over Brook for a split second, softening slightly when they landed on her tear-streaked face before hardening again as they locked onto the irate man.

"Back the fuck away from her. Now."

The man froze, his mouth opening as though to protest, but no sound came out. Storm's glare and imposing stance were enough to silence whatever argument was on the tip of his tongue.

Scowling, the man's face darkened like a brewing storm as he stepped back, huffing and puffing in frustration, his chest rising and falling with exaggerated indignation. He looked ready to blow someone's house down, his irritation almost comical if the situation weren't so tense.

"This lady can't drive! That's what's going on!" he snapped, his voice laced with bitterness, though under Storm's unrelenting glare, it lacked the bluster and bravado it had moments earlier.

Brook stood frozen, her heart hammering against her ribs. She didn't trust herself to speak; her throat felt too tight, and she was sure her voice would crack if she tried. She didn't move, didn't trust her shaky legs to keep her standing with all the anger flying around. Confrontation was scary at the best of times, and this wasn't the best of times.

Storm's sharp gaze softened the instant it shifted to her. "You okay, sunshine?" he asked gently, ignoring the man entirely as though he were nothing more than background noise.

She nodded quickly, then shook her head, her emotions tangling in a whirlwind. "I—I think so," she stammered, her voice trembling. "He hit me when I stopped for the red light."

Storm's jaw tightened, the muscle twitching as anger simmered just beneath the surface. He turned his attention back to the man, his expression hard and unyielding. "So, you rear-ended her, which makes it your fault, asshole." Each of his words were clipped and deliberate.

The man's mouth opened, but whatever excuse or retort he had prepared withered. "Whatever," he muttered finally, waving a dismissive hand as he turned toward his car. "Let's just exchange insurance details and get this over with."

Storm didn't move until the man had stalked off, chundering under his breath. Only then did he step closer to Brook, his towering frame offering a protective shield. His eyes softened again as he took in her trembling hands, the faint sheen of tears still lingering in her eyes. "You sure you're okay, baby?" he asked, barely above a murmur.

Brook glanced down at her hands, realizing for the first time how much she was shaking. When he gently wrapped his much larger hands around hers, the warmth of his touch steadied her, if only slightly. "I'm fine," she whispered, but the wavering in her voice betrayed her.

Storm frowned, his dark eyes scanning her face as if searching for a lie. "Come on," he said quietly, tilting his head toward his truck. "I'll take you back to my place. You don't look like you should be driving right now."

"What about my car?" she asked, her voice small. There was some damage to the back of the car, and Brook didn't want to leave it out in the open where someone else could hit it.

"I'll pull it into that parking lot over there and have a couple of the guys come pick it up," he assured her, in a composed but firm tone. "Don't worry about it, Little one. I'll handle all of this. Let's just get you in my truck where it's warm and you can sit down."

Too drained to argue, she let him guide her to the passenger seat. Before she knew it, he was leaning over her, buckling her in with smooth, practiced motions. His presence was like a blanket of calm, the faint scent of leather and soap grounding her as he got her situated.

"Wait here," he commanded gently. "All your insurance stuff is in the glove box?"

She nodded, and he closed the door softly, leaving her alone to watch as he approached the other driver, who was waiting by the side of the road, clutching his paperwork. Storm's posture was confident, his movements precise, and even from a distance, she could see how he handled the situation with a cool, unshakable authority that was both reassuring and captivating.

Twenty minutes later, Storm climbed into the driver's

seat, her purse and cell phone in hand. He gave them to her without a word before starting the engine. The silence in the truck was heavy but comforting, broken only by the faint hum of the heater. Every few minutes, he glanced her way, his dark eyes checking her carefully, as though making sure she wasn't falling apart.

Brook sank deeper into the seat, her body and mind finally starting to relax. She didn't know what she'd done to deserve someone like Storm showing up when she needed him most, but for now, she let herself feel safe.

When they finally pulled up to the clubhouse, Storm moved with his usual calm efficiency, but there was an extra layer of gentleness in his actions. He opened her door, reaching in to unbuckle her seatbelt and lift her effortlessly from the seat, cradling her as though she were made of glass before setting her on her feet. His arms were strong and steady, a reassuring anchor in the whirlwind of her emotions. Without a word, he guided her inside, his large hand resting lightly on her back as they moved through the common area.

Storm exchanged a few brief words with some of the club members they passed, his tone firm and no-nonsense, but Brook barely processed what he said. Everything around her felt muffled, distant. Maybe she was in shock— her mind still caught in the chaos of the crash. All she knew was that she was profoundly grateful Storm was there, his presence grounding her when everything else felt like it was about to spiral out of control.

When they reached a small, cozy apartment, he closed the door firmly behind them and turned the lock with a decisive click. He crossed to the couch, grabbed a soft, well-worn blanket, and draped it gently over her shoulders. Then he crouched in front of her, bringing his dark, steady eyes level with hers. His gaze held a quiet intensity, a silent promise that nothing would harm her here.

"You're safe," he said, his voice low and soothing, the words wrapping around her like the blanket, adding an extra level of security that she desperately needed. "And I'm not going anywhere, okay?"

The tight knot that had been coiled in her chest since the crash loosened slightly, and for the first time, she felt her lungs expand fully as she exhaled. Relief washed over her in waves.

"Thank you," she murmured, barely above a whisper. "I'm sorry if I ruined your plans or whatever you were doing."

Her eyes flicked over him, taking in the fitted navy-blue Henley that stretched across his broad chest and the dark jeans that hugged his muscular frame. Some of his tattoos peeked out of the bottom of his sleeves, which she found she liked. He looked impossibly good—more polished than usual. A sudden zing of jealousy sparked through her, irrational but insistent. Had he been on his way to meet someone? A date, maybe?

Storm settled onto the couch next to her, close enough that their thighs brushed. The warmth of his presence was immediate, calming. He took her hand in his, his thumb gently stroking over her knuckles as he spoke. "I'd just come from a meeting at my bank about the loan for the house I'm buying," he explained, his tone even and reassuring. "I was headed to your office to try and catch you before the end of the work-day. I wanted to ask you to dinner and a movie to celebrate my offer being accepted."

Her mouth fell open slightly, surprise flickering across her face. "You were coming to see me?"

His dark eyes stayed locked on hers as he nodded, and a warm flutter spread through her chest. In the three days since their lunch date, she hadn't been able to stop thinking about Storm. She'd worried when they didn't exchange numbers, worrying that perhaps he wasn't as interested as she'd hoped. But now, knowing he'd been seeking her out, those doubts melted away.

"I'm sorry I ruined it," she said softly though her words were tinged with regret.

Storm didn't reply immediately. Instead, he reached over and scooped her up with effortless strength, settling her onto his lap. She gasped softly, startled by the ease with which he lifted her, but being surrounded by his warmth and solidity quickly calmed her. Compared to him, she felt small—a rare and oddly comforting sensation.

"You didn't ruin it, sunshine." His arms tightened around her, his hold protective as he continued in a low rumble, "Scared me a bit. I didn't like seeing you out there on your own with that asshole yelling at you. That fucker needs his ass kicked."

A soft smile touched her lips, and she leaned her head against his chest, listening to the steady beat of his heart. "Thank you for saving me."

He didn't respond with words, but he didn't need to. Instead, his arms tightened around her more securely, his embrace a silent reassurance. He reclined against the couch, reaching for the remote, and turned on the flat-screen TV. The cheerful opening notes of *Bluey* filled the room, and Brook blinked, her heart lifting a little. He couldn't have known it, but it was one of her favorite cartoons—light, playful, and exactly what she needed to decompress from the chaos of the day.

Storm rested his chin lightly on the top of her head, his steadiness grounding her in ways she didn't realize were possible. For the first time all day, she felt truly at ease, safe in the quiet warmth of his company.

It didn't take long before her eyes felt too heavy to keep open and she let herself fade to sleep in the security and comfort of Storm's arms.

Brook woke up, still safe in Storm's arms, her thumb lodged in her mouth and a blanket covering her. She blinked several times, trying to quiet the swirl of emotions inside her. Storm's breathing was shallow and even, so she was pretty sure he had fallen asleep, too. She was happy to have a moment of privacy to think about everything that had happened over the past few hours. The accident had been minor, and yet she'd completely panicked. If Storm hadn't shown up, she wasn't sure what would have happened. It wasn't worth thinking about what that man could have done. But then Storm took over and cared for her in such a gentle way that surprised her.

Needing to use the bathroom, she tried to scoot off his

lap, but he tightened his arms around her. "Where are you going, sunshine?"

A smile tugged at her lips, and she tilted her head to look up at him. His eyes were closed, but then he opened them just slightly and peered down at her.

"I need to go to the bathroom." Her voice was small, and heat crept up her checks.

"I guess I'll allow it." As he loosened his grip and winked, she awkwardly stood. "Do you need help in there, baby?"

*What?*

Help in the bathroom?

What would she need help with?

The idea definitely did something to her, and she was suddenly glad to be on her feet. It would be really embarrassing to leave a wet spot on his jeans.

"No. I'm good."

He quirked his mouth and pointed toward an open door. "It's in there. Wash your hands when you're done. I'm going to make you something warm to drink."

Storm was walking back to the couch when she returned with two mugs in his hands.

"Thank you," she murmured as she sat down. "For stopping, for… just… everything. I don't know what I'd have done if you hadn't shown up."

"Hey," he said softly, setting one of the drinks on a side table. "You don't have to thank me. You looked like you needed someone, and I wasn't about to let you deal with that jerk alone."

They stared at each other for a long moment before he lowered himself next to her. "Drink this. Hot chocolate fixes everything. Be careful, though, it might be too hot. Wait, let me test it first. I don't want you to burn yourself." Before she could take it from him, he brought the mug to his lips, tipping it back for a drink. When he was happy it wasn't going to hurt her, Storm passed Brook the cup. She giggled. He certainly was overprotective.

She hummed as she took a drink. "It's so good."

Storm winked at her then sat back and watched *Peppa Pig* with her like it was his favorite show. Surely, he wasn't enjoying this.

"You smell nice," she said suddenly, surprising herself.

He chuckled, the low sound vibrating through her. "Yeah? I wanted to say the same thing about you. Caramel and vanilla. Fucking edible."

Her cheeks grew hot, and she avoided his gaze for a few seconds, then looked up at him. He was watching her, his eyes intense but not overwhelming, like he was trying to read every thought she wasn't saying out loud.

The air between them crackled, and almost like a magnet was pulling her, she leaned closer to him. Storm gently set his cup on the side table then took hers and did the same. She didn't understand how she could be so aroused by someone just from being in their presence, but it was instant when she was around him. Her core ached, and her breasts were heavy. She wanted him.

After a moment, he lowered his face to hers, his lips brushing hers delicately at first, as though giving her a chance to pull away. When she didn't, he deepened the kiss, his hand sliding up to cup her cheek.

Storm's kiss was everything Brook hadn't realized she was waiting for—a slow, deliberate unraveling of restraint.

Her heart thudded against her ribcage as his hand moved from her cheek to cradle the nape of her neck, his thumb tracing lazy circles against her skin. She melted into him, her fingers clutching the fabric of his shirt like it was a lifeline.

When he finally pulled back, her breath came in short, uneven bursts, her chest rising and falling against his. His dark gaze locked onto hers, intense but devoid of danger. Instead, it held something far more alluring, far more potent—a magnetic pull that left her dizzy.

"Brook," he muttered, his voice gravelly and thick with emotion.

"Yeah?" Her words came out barely more than a whisper, trembling slightly as her fingers relaxed their grip on him.

He smirked then, that signature Storm confidence flickering in the curve of his lips, but there was a softness behind it that wasn't usually there. "I've wanted to kiss you since the first day we met. You have no idea how hard it's been holding back."

"Really?" she replied, even quieter this time.

"Yeah, sunshine." His gaze dropped briefly to her lips before meeting her eyes again. "Fuck, I wanted to kiss you the night I followed you home, but I didn't want to scare you."

The sincerity in his tone, the way his words carried no hint of regret, sent a warm shiver coursing through her. His openness was disarming, but it made her feel safe and cherished in a way she hadn't expected.

"You don't scare me," she told him, her voice steadier now.

Storm's smile widened, the warmth in his expression softening the hard edges of his face. He leaned down, pressing a lingering kiss to her forehead, the tenderness of the gesture making her heart squeeze. Then he settled back into the couch, pulling her closer until she was nestled snugly against him, her head resting against his chest.

"I'm glad, baby girl," he murmured in a soothing rumble that vibrated through her.

In his arms, with his steady heartbeat beneath her ear and his warmth enveloping her, everything else seemed to fade away. It was a moment she never wanted to end.

# SEVEN
## STORM

She fit against him so perfectly it was almost maddening. Every soft curve of Brook's soft, lush body molded seamlessly to the hard lines of his muscular frame, as though she'd been made to rest there. Storm couldn't ignore the quiet certainty settling deep in his chest—a primal understanding that she was *his*. But that fucked-up voice in his mind wouldn't let him bask in the thought for long. It whispered continuous doubts, telling him he wasn't the kind of man she'd want or need.

He'd seen the way she watched his friends with their Littles, her eyes lighting up with interest and longing. She liked how they cared for the girls—gentle, doting, patient. But Storm? He wasn't any of those things. He was rough around the edges, gruff, and prone to long stretches of silence. A self-proclaimed hermit. He wasn't built for soft words and nurturing touches. She deserved better than him—someone brighter and more open.

He knew it, but even so, he couldn't make himself walk away from her.

"I need to feed you and get you home," he said thickly, breaking the silence.

Brook tilted her head up, her green eyes locking onto his. "What about my car? Do you think it's drivable? It wasn't that hard of a hit."

He set her carefully on her feet and rose, towering over her as he reached for her hand, his touch firm but warm. "It's drivable, but I want to check it out in the shop tomorrow to make sure it's safe," he replied, leaving no room for argument.

As he led her from the apartment toward the community kitchen, she stayed quiet, her fingers curling around his as they walked. But the moment they stepped inside and she spotted Carlee, Brook's demeanor shifted completely, her Little side bubbling to the surface like she couldn't contain it any longer.

"Oh my gosh, I'm so glad you're okay!" Carlee squealed, rushing toward her and throwing her arms around Brook in a dramatic hug. "Daddy said you were in a car accident."

She nodded, but her gaze flicked upward, seeking Storm's eyes. The look she gave him, soft and full of trust, warmed him from the inside out, a feeling he couldn't quite put into words. He liked that. A lot. She was asking for his reassurance, leaning on him in a way that stirred something deep and protective within him.

"She needs to eat," he grunted at the Littles, gently nudging Brook toward the table, steering her away from Carlee's whirlwind of energy.

"Gabriel made chili and cornbread for dinner. It's in the crockpot," Atlas called out, glancing up from the sink where he was washing dishes.

"Thanks," Storm replied, his voice curt but appreciative. He pulled out a chair for Brook, waiting patiently for her to sit before pushing her in with deliberate care. Leaning down, he brought his mouth close to her ear, speaking softly. "Do you want milk or water, sunshine?"

She nibbled on her bottom lip, her teeth tugging at the soft flesh as uncertainty flickered across her face. He recognized her hesitation immediately and cursed himself silently. Making decisions wasn't easy for her Little—it overwhelmed her.

"I'll get you milk," he said gently, straightening and brushing a hand lightly across her shoulder. "Stay right here, Little one."

Her shoulders relaxed and the relief in her expression was subtle but unmistakable, and it hit him like a punch to the gut. She trusted him to take care of her, and for once, he didn't second-guess his ability to do so. He glanced back toward the table, his gaze settling on her. Brook sat quietly, her hands resting on her lap, but her eyes never left him, filled with something that made his chest ache.

She didn't just trust him—she *wanted* him. And that made all the difference.

Atlas followed Storm into the kitchen, moving with his usual easygoing confidence. He opened the fridge, grabbed a beer, and held one up as an offer. Storm shook his head. One beer wouldn't affect him, but he still needed to get Brook home. With her in his care, he wasn't taking any chances. Her safety came first, always.

"You okay? You seem pretty tense," Atlas said, tossing the bottle cap into the garbage with a practiced flick before leaning casually against the counter. His sharp eyes watched Storm fill two bowls with steaming chili. The rich, savory aroma filled the room, a reminder that Gabriel truly was the best damn cook in the clubhouse.

"I'm fine," Storm replied gruffly, his tone clipped as he focused on his task.

Atlas smirked knowingly, taking a swig from his beer. "You don't seem fine."

Storm's gaze snapped up, his dark eyes narrowing in a glare. "When did you become such a nosy fuck? I said I'm fine."

For a moment, the two friends locked eyes, the tension between them thick. But then Storm exhaled heavily, his broad shoulders sagging as he rubbed at his temples. "She could have gotten really fucking hurt. And on top of that, the asshole who ran into her was in her face, screaming like a damn lunatic."

Atlas was quiet for a beat, sipping his beer thoughtfully. "It scared you," he said finally, his voice calm but laced with understanding.

Damn right, it scared him. The admission churned in Storm's gut, unsettling him. He wasn't used to feeling like this—so out of control, so raw. Caring about someone wasn't second nature to him. It was terrifying. But the need to protect Brook, to shield her from anything and everything, burned inside him like a relentless fire. He wanted to be her protector, her safe place. Like a Daddy should be.

"Why are you being so fucking stubborn about admitting you like her?" Atlas's question blunt but not unkind.

Storm's hands stilled as he poured milk into a sippy cup, his jaw tightening. Twisting the lid on firmly, he answered without looking up. "Because she deserves someone way better than me."

Atlas scoffed, setting his beer down with a *thunk*. "Who would be better than you?" he challenged, his voice cutting through Storm's self-doubt. "The Storm I know is loyal, protective, and caring—in your own fucked-up way. Do you really think anyone would Daddy her better than you?"

Storm opened his mouth to respond, but Atlas didn't wait for an answer. With a parting glance, he pushed off the counter and strolled out of the kitchen, leaving Storm alone to stew in his thoughts.

The truth hit hard. Storm couldn't stand the idea of any other man touching Brook. The thought of someone else's hands on her soft, curvy body filled him with a possessive rage he couldn't ignore. But would she want that? Could she handle who he was—the rough edges, the gruff demeanor, the absolute need to protect her in *every* way possible? He wasn't going to change; he'd tried that before, bending and twisting himself into someone he wasn't for his ex. And she'd cheated on him anyway, leaving him bitter and wary.

Unease prickled at the back of his neck as he picked up the bowls of chili and carried them to the table where Brook sat waiting. She looked up at him with those emerald-green eyes, trusting and innocent, and his chest tightened. This wasn't something he needed to figure out tonight. But even as he sat across from her, the urge to claim her as his, to make sure everyone knew she belonged to him, gnawed at him relentlessly.

For now, he pushed those thoughts aside. He didn't need all the answers tonight—but he knew one thing for certain: he wasn't letting Brook go.

"It's hot, Little one. Don't eat it yet," Storm cautioned, his deep voice firm yet gentle as he rose from his chair and headed back to the kitchen. His broad shoulders seemed to block out the room as he moved, grabbing a plate of corn-bread and her sippy cup of milk.

When he returned, he settled into the chair beside her. She turned slightly toward him, her soft green eyes lifting to meet his. "Thank you," she said quietly, her voice laced with warmth.

"You're welcome." His lips twitched into a faint smile before he asked, "Do you want me to feed you?"

The question hung in the air, and Storm tried to keep his expression neutral, though the thought of pulling her onto his lap and spoon-feeding her sent a flicker of heat through his body. He wasn't sure if she'd be comfortable with it, and the last thing he wanted was to push her too far, too fast. So, he gave her the choice, even though his instincts screamed to take over.

"Um," she murmured, glancing around the room where a handful of club members lingered. Her cheeks flushed faintly. "I can do it."

He nodded, keeping his disappointment at bay, and tested the temperature of his chili before handing her a thick-handled plastic spoon. They ate in silence, the quiet between them feeling more intimate than awkward. Every so often, Brook took a drink from the sippy cup he'd set in front of her, the action both innocent and endearing. Carlee and Atlas had disappeared, and the other Littles were nowhere to be seen, leaving the two of them in a comfortable bubble of solitude.

By the time they finished their dinner, Brook looked utterly spent. Her eyelids drooped, and her posture relaxed into a quiet lethargy. When she let out a yawn, Storm's protective instincts kicked in, his mind racing with the desire to bring her to his apartment and tuck her into his bed. She'd been in a car accident, minor or not, and the thought of her out of his sight made his jaw tighten.

But if he put her in his bed... he wasn't sure he'd ever be able to let her leave. The idea of her small, warm body curled up in his sheets was almost too much to bear. His cock ached, and every time she walked in front of him, his gaze trailed to her ass—round, plump, and *perfect*. He couldn't fathom how she didn't already have a Daddy. The thought of another man with her made his fists clench— thank fuck she was unattached. If she weren't, Storm wasn't entirely sure he wouldn't resort to something drastic to claim her.

After they climbed into his truck and headed toward her apartment, he tried to focus on making conversation, something he'd never been particularly good at. "How did you meet Carlee?" he asked, keeping his eyes on the road but sneaking a glance at her from the corner of his eye.

"At the library," she replied softly, her voice as soothing as the night itself.

He arched a brow and glanced at her for a moment before returning his attention to the road. "The library?

People actually *meet* there? I thought it was all old books and forced silence."

Her lips curved into a faint smile, one that seemed almost indulgent, like she was humoring him. "Well, that's part of the charm. Quiet corners, shelves full of stories, and no one really expects you to talk to them. Except Carlee. She was determined to be my friend once she found out we like to read the same books."

Storm chuckled under his breath, which rumbled in the quiet of the truck. He didn't say it, but he was grateful Carlee had been persistent. Because if she hadn't, he might never have met Brook. And the thought of never knowing her, never having the chance to hold her, to care for her—it wasn't a world he wanted to imagine.

He nodded, even though he wasn't entirely sure how to respond. "What do you guys read? Like, book club kind of stuff or…?"

She laughed lightly, and he was pretty sure if it wasn't dark out he'd see a blush rising on her cheeks.

"Not exactly. We, uh, we read romance."

He was pretty sure she wasn't telling him the entire truth, but he didn't want to embarrass her.

"Sounds like fun," he said, although he couldn't remember the last time he'd picked up a book that wasn't some kind of engine manual.

When Storm pulled into one of the visitor parking spots near Brook's apartment, he cut the engine and let the low growl of the truck fade into silence. He glanced at her, his almost-black eyes searching her face. *Fuck. What now?*

"What time do you work in the morning?" he asked, his voice gruff but soft enough not to scare her off.

She turned those sparkling green eyes to him, nibbling on her bottom lip in a way that made his chest tighten. "Eight," she said softly.

He nodded, already making plans in his head. "I'll be here at seven-thirty to pick you up."

Her eyes widened in surprise, and she shook her head quickly. "No, Storm. You've done enough already. I'll take the bus."

His nostrils flared as irritation spiked through him. He didn't like hearing his name roll off her tongue like that. The only thing he wanted her to call him was *Daddy*. He leaned in slightly, his voice low and commanding. "You get on a bus, and you'll be in trouble, sunshine. Got me?"

The tension between them crackled, an invisible current charging the air. She held his gaze, her lips parting slightly, and he could feel himself teetering on the edge. Would taking a chance with her really be so bad?

"You're not my Daddy," she whispered, trembling but defiant. "You can't tell me what to do."

That made him laugh, a deep, gravelly sound that filled the cab of the truck. When he stopped, he raised a brow, daring her to defy him further. She licked her lips nervously, the motion drawing his attention like a magnet.

"Sunshine," his words were smooth and deliberate, "I may not be your Daddy, but I sure as hell can tell you what to do when it comes to your safety. And you're going to be a good girl and obey me, aren't you?"

*Fuck.* The way she pulled her plump bottom lip between her teeth made him lose the tenuous grip he had on his restraint. Without thinking, he reached over, his rough thumb tugging her delicate lip free. A small, breathy whimper escaped her, and that was it. He was so totally gone for her.

She wasn't like Emmaline—she wasn't manipulative or demanding. Brook was different. She was genuinely Little, sweet as sugar and so damn sincere it made his chest ache.

"Maybe I *should* be your Daddy," he rasped. The atmosphere in the cab suddenly became thick with emotion. "I think you need one."

Being vulnerable wasn't easy for him, but he couldn't fight the feelings surging inside him any longer. He *wanted* to be her Daddy. To care for her, protect her, make her laugh, and keep her safe. To make her *happy.*

"I can take care of myself, thank you very much," she replied, lifting her chin in a stubborn challenge.

He couldn't help but chuckle, his lips twitching. "Really, sunshine? What time did you go to bed last night? Or all week, for that matter? How about dinner? What did you eat other than nuggets and ranch?"

Her cheeks turned a fiery red, confirming everything he suspected. She shifted in her seat. "I didn't say I was very good at it," she admitted, her lips twitching with a reluctant smile.

Storm reached out, pinching her chin gently between his fingers. His dark gaze bore into hers as he spoke. "You've been doing just fine for a Little girl trying to do it all herself. But I can do it better, and I think you need that. Want that, even. I see how you watch the other Littles."

Her eyes sparkled, and she swallowed thickly. "Maybe," she murmured. "But I'm different from them."

He leaned closer, resting his forehead against hers. "I know that, sunshine. It's why I like you so much. I'm different, too. I'm grumpy, controlling, bossy, and I like to be alone more often than not. Except with you—I like being with you."

A slow grin spread across her lips, lighting up her face in a way that made his heart stumble. "I like being with you, too."

"Good," he said, his voice softening. "So, what do you say, Little one? Would you like me to be your Daddy?"

When she hesitated, his heart felt like it had stopped in his chest. The silence stretched, each second an eternity, until finally, she nodded.

"Okay," she said quietly. "Let's try it."

Relief and a fierce sense of possessiveness surged through him, so strong it nearly left him breathless. Brook had no idea just how much she meant to him already, but he'd make sure she knew. And he'd make sure he was the best damn Daddy possible for her.

# EIGHT
## BROOK

She couldn't believe she'd agreed to it. The word "okay" had left her lips before she could fully process what it meant, and now her heart was racing and her mind spinning. What shocked her even more was that Storm had *asked*. For a man so confident and commanding, he could have just told her how things would be, and yet, he hadn't. His consideration made her chest ache in a way she didn't entirely understand.

There was no denying the connection between them, an almost magnetic pull that had been there since the first time he'd walked into the real estate office. Even through his disapproving looks, she'd felt it between them. The way his dark eyes would narrow at her, the subtle clench of his jaw—it had sent a thrill through her that was both exhilarating and nerve-wracking. Being near him was like standing too close to a fire, tempting and dangerous.

"What do we do now?" she asked, quiet but steady, even as her pulse hammered in her ears.

Storm's smile was slow, deliberate, and devastatingly warm. His hand remained firm on her chin, his thumb brushing against her jaw, sending heat coursing through her. "Now," he said, sounding steady and commanding, "you go inside, get ready for bed, and go to sleep. No reading, no playing, *and* no touching yourself."

Her cheeks flared with so much heat she was sure they were glowing. If it were possible to spontaneously combust from sheer embarrassment, this would be the moment. She reacted instantly to his words in her core, flipping and twisting in ways she didn't know it could. Her panties had been damp since the moment he swooped in at the accident scene and took control. Brook thought she'd known what it was like to be turned on, but this— this was an entirely new level. Storm had awakened something inside her that no one else had ever come close to touching.

"The blush on your cheeks tells me you might have been thinking about doing the last part, sunshine," he teased, his voice dipping lower, velvet and steel all at once.

*Damn.* How did he read her so effortlessly? It was both maddening and thrilling.

"I was not," she whispered, though her words lacked conviction.

He chuckled, the deep, rumble vibrating through her like a physical touch. He leaned in closer, his dark eyes locking onto hers with an intensity that stole her breath. "Just so you know, Little girls who lie to me get put over Daddy's lap, their panties pulled down to their knees, and their adorable bottoms spanked. Do you want to make a trip across my lap tonight, baby?"

*Oh. God.*

Her thoughts scrambled. Did she? The answer was an overwhelming, contradictory *yes*—and also a panicked, *heck, no.*

The idea of being spanked by Storm, with his enormous, powerful hands, was as thrilling as it was terrifying. She could already imagine the heat, the sting, the way his strength would make her feel small and safe all at once. But she also wanted to be able to sit comfortably at her desk tomorrow.

"No, thank you," she managed to squeak, her voice barely above a whisper.

His chuckle was rich with amusement, his lips curling into a smirk that made her knees weak. "So polite," he murmured, winking at her. "Using your manners to get out of a spanking, sunshine."

Her heart fluttered wildly. This man was going to be the death of her, and she wasn't sure if she cared one bit.

"I will be at your place in the morning to pick you up. Wear a thick coat, it's going to be cold."

She sighed, bummed that this moment was coming to an end. Spending time with Storm was addicting.

"I hate that you have to come all the way back here tomorrow. Are you sure you don't want to stay? You can sleep in my bed, and I can sleep on the couch."

For some reason, she knew that was the wrong thing to say because his jaw clenched, and his eyes darkened even more. "Little girl, if you ever think I would allow you to sleep on any couch, you'd be sadly mistaken. And as much as I'd love to come in and sleep in bed with you, I don't think it's a good idea."

Eyebrows pinched, she tilted her head to the side. "Why not?"

Storm shifted uncomfortably, and when she flicked her eyes down, she gasped. Even though it was dark in the cab of his truck, there was enough light for her to catch the outline of something long and hard pressing against his jeans. Had *she* done that to him?

"Because I'm barely holding on by a thread as it is, sunshine. Today was an emotional day, and it's already late. I want you to get a full eight hours of sleep. What kind of Daddy would I be if I kept you up all night?"

The best kind. Not that she would ever say that out loud. But she did like the thought of all the things Storm might do to her. She had a feeling he wasn't a missionary kind of man like her exes had been.

"Oh," is all she said.

"I don't want to send you in there alone, though, if you're still upset." He ran his thumb over the apple of her cheek.

She leaned into his touch. They'd agreed he would be her Daddy, but she didn't know what that meant exactly. So many unanswered questions would keep her up half the night. That was what she was a mess over. The accident was already forgotten.

"I'm okay. I was more shaken up by the guy screaming at me. I don't like it when people yell."

"Understandable, baby girl. I don't like it either, and I sure as fuck don't like it when they do it to you. I'd still debating showing up to that asshole's house to teach him a lesson."

It was ridiculous to be touched by the fact that Storm

wanted to protect her, but her heart still fluttered wildly. "You already took care of everything. I'm okay."

The tension behind his gaze faded slightly at her reassurance. "I'll walk you to your door."

Nodding, she reached for the handle to climb out of the truck, but he grabbed her arm, stopping her. "Don't ever open your own door when we're together, sunshine. That's my job now. Wait for me."

Then he rounded the front and pulled it open for her. He held out his hands, and when she put hers in his larger ones, he helped her climb out until her feet settled on the ground. Sheesh. Who made those things so tall? They were not fit for someone short like her.

"Thank you."

Without letting go, Storm led her up the walkway and then stood behind her protectively as she fished her keys out. When she turned to face him, his nearly black eyes met hers, sparkling with what she was sure was arousal.

"What are you going to do when I leave?" he asked quietly.

He was testing her. He had told her in the truck what he'd wanted her to do, but she had to search her mind to try to remember. Everything was so fuzzy when she was around him. She was also distracted by the knowledge that his cock was hard.

"Um, bed?"

The corner of his mouth quirked into a smirk. "My girl might need to work on her listening skills, huh?"

"Um..."

Storm chuckled and hooked his index finger under her chin. "You're going to lock this door when I leave, and then you're going to get ready for bed. Brush your teeth, drink some water, get into pajamas, and crawl into bed. When you're tucked in, I want you to text and let me know. Got it?"

She nodded and then opened her mouth to speak, but he held out a card before she could get it out. "Here's my number. Steele's number is also on this card along with Kade and Bear's. If you ever can't get hold of me and you need help, you call any of them. Okay?"

The crisp card had a bear logo on the front with all four men's names on the back and their phone numbers. It looked much more official than she would have expected for a motorcycle club.

"Put mine into your phone and text me right now so I can save your info," he told her.

He waited patiently as she did so. When his phone pinged, he nodded and then stepped forward, sliding his hand behind her neck. "That's my good girl. I'll talk to you soon."

Before she could agree, he leaned down and brushed his lips over hers. Goosebumps rose over her arms as she kissed him back, her arms snaking around his waist. He was so tall compared to her, but it didn't seem to deter him. Instead, he rested one palm on the door frame and held her firmly as he dominated her mouth with his.

It was demanding. Precise. At the same time, it was intimate. Exploring. Not rushed in the slightest. Storm seemed like the type of man who might be impatient, but not with her. He always took his time.

When he pulled back, they stared at each other for a

long moment before he cleared his throat. "Lock this door, sunshine."

Then he stepped out of the way to let her shut him out, his gaze locked with hers until they were unable to see each other. She set the deadbolt and rose to her tiptoes to watch Storm walk away through the peephole.

Wow.

That was… *intense.*

Resting her hand over her racing heart, Brook sighed and blinked several times.

She could hardly wait to talk to Carlee about this. It would have to wait until tomorrow, though. Her Daddy had given her tasks to do, and she didn't want to be naughty right out of the gate.

Storm arrived at her door at exactly seven-thirty, punctual to the last second. When Brook opened it, the sight of him stole her breath. The fitted, white Henley he wore clung to his broad chest and muscular shoulders, the fabric stretched just enough to hint at the tattoos winding up his forearms. It made her mouth go dry the instant she let him in, and she had to remind herself to breathe.

"Carlee told me you like chai tea," he said, holding out a cup from the local coffee shop. "I told them not to make it too hot, but I didn't trust them, so I tried it to make sure it wouldn't burn you."

Her eyes widened, her gaze darting from the steaming

cup to his dark, steady eyes. Staring up at him, her lips parted in surprise. "That's... really considerate." She spoke so quietly her words came out on a breath.

As she took the cup, her fingers brushed his, and for a fleeting moment, her brain seemed to short-circuit.

*Get it together. You cannot get all hot and bothered over him testing your drink.*

Storm shrugged, the movement casual, and his lips curved into a slight smirk. "Don't worry," he said, leaning against the door frame with an effortless confidence that made her knees feel weak. "I didn't drink much. Just enough to be a hero."

*Was he being funny?* Brook blinked. *Does Storm actually have a sense of humor?*

She giggled, rolling her eyes dramatically. "Oh, a hero, huh? Did you save kittens from trees on the way here, too?"

"No trees," he replied smoothly, his tone full of mock seriousness. "But I did help an adorable Little girl yesterday who was in a minor accident. It's all in a day's work."

Brook shook her head, trying to stifle her smile as she stepped back to let him inside. "Come in, Mr. Hero. I'm not awake enough for all this charm."

He followed her, his dark gaze sweeping over her apartment. Though most of her Little things were tidied away in her bedroom, there were a few touches scattered throughout the main living area—a pastel throw blanket draped over the couch, a jar of crayons sitting on a stack of coloring books on the coffee table, and a plush unicorn perched on a shelf. Subtle but telling.

"I like your place, sunshine," he said genuinely. "It's cute. Just like you."

Her heart gave an unsteady flutter at the sweetness and sincerity of his words. It was such a simple compliment, yet it sent warmth spreading through her chest like sunlight breaking through clouds. She shouldn't have been so affected, but it wasn't even eight in the morning, and she was already dangerously close to becoming putty in his hands.

"Thank you," she murmured, her cheeks pink. "I just need to grab my bag."

"No rush," he said, his tone easy.

She ducked into her bedroom, grabbing her work stuff and taking a moment to double-check her appearance in the mirror. When she returned, she found Storm standing in front of one of her bookshelves. The one filled with her collection of smutty, filthy comfort reads. The color drained from her face, only to be replaced by a fiery blush when he turned toward her, a knowing gleam in his eyes.

Her stomach flipped as she ducked her head, her whole body blazing. *Of all the shelves...*

Storm chuckled softly and closed the distance between them, his movements slow and deliberate. Gently but still firm, he cupped her chin, tilting her face up so she had no choice but to meet his gaze.

"Don't be embarrassed about what you read, sunshine," he murmured, his deep voice laced with amusement and something far more seductive. "It's hot. I like knowing you read these books. Maybe one of these nights, I can read to you before bed."

Brook swallowed hard, the image of his suggestion

making her pulse race. She wasn't sure she'd survive the experience without bursting into flames, but his easy acceptance of her book choices sent a wave of relief crashing over her.

His thumb brushed her cheek in a tender, almost absentminded motion, the casual intimacy of it making her knees wobble. Her voice was almost trapped in her throat, her ability to think slipping away under his penetrating gaze. All she could do was look up at him, her heart hammering against her ribcage as he smiled, clearly aware of the effect he had on her.

"We're going to be late," she muttered breathily.

"Okay, sunshine. Let's go."

They drove in silence through their small town as shop owners turned their closed signs to open, set up produce and other items on the sidewalks, started their day with the sunrise coming over the horizon. Brook had lived here all her life. She loved this place, it was her home.

Brook glanced at him as they walked hand in hand, her curiosity getting the better of her. "How long have you lived in Shadowridge?" she asked, her voice soft but filled with interest.

Storm turned his head slightly, his thumb brushing idly over the back of her hand, sending a little spark through her. "All my life," he replied simply. "My father was the VP of the MC."

"And now you are?" she prompted, tilting her head to look at him.

"Yeah," he confirmed, his tone steady. "Now I am."

"Do you like it?" she asked with genuine curiosity.

Without hesitation, he nodded. "I do. The guys are my

brothers. My family. They don't expect me to be anyone I'm not."

That caught her attention, and she couldn't help but wonder what he meant. Who would ask him to be someone else? From what she'd seen, Storm was perfect just as he was—confident, protective, and unapologetically himself.

"Do you have any other family?" she asked after a pause, her voice gentler this time.

"My mom still lives in town," he said with his gaze fixed ahead. "My pop died a long time ago." His grip on her hand tightened slightly before he turned the question back on her. "What about you? Who do you have in your life?"

A pang of sadness squeezed deep in her chest, but she forced the best smile she could muster. "My mom lives here, too. So, I have her. And Carlee too, I guess."

Storm glanced at her sharply, and she hated the way admitting that made her feel so... alone. Like she wasn't enough. Like she was some kind of loser.

"Yeah, I'd say you have Carlee and *all* the other Littles," he said firmly. "And you have me now. Plus, that includes the rest of the MC. So, I'd say you have a whole lot of people in your life, sunshine."

Brook's breath hitched, and for a moment, she didn't know what to say. A lump formed in her throat, and it was probably for the best that she stayed silent. She wasn't sure she'd be able to speak past the overwhelming warmth his kind words brought.

"I don't know how we've never run into each other before," Storm added, his tone softer now, almost contemplative. "Fucking shame it took us so long to meet."

For someone so gruff, even with his frequent swearing, Storm had a surprising way of saying the sweetest things. It left her feeling both flustered and giddy at once.

When he pulled into the parking lot of her office, Brook hesitated to touch the handle of the truck door, remembering what he'd said last night about her not opening doors when he was with her. She peeked at him from beneath her lashes, and he dipped his chin in approval. "Good girl," he praised with a smile.

Her heart fluttered wildly, and she couldn't suppress the faint shiver that ran through her. Going to work with soaked panties hadn't been part of her plan for the day, but apparently, it was inevitable now Storm was her Daddy.

"Thank you for driving me to work," she murmured as he helped her down from the truck. "I'm sorry to put you out."

Storm's eyes softened, though his lips twitched into a smirk. "You didn't *put me out*, sunshine," he said sincerely. "This is the best fucking way to start the day if you ask me."

Her cheeks heated at his words, and she couldn't help but smile. "You really do swear a lot," she teased, her tone light.

He raised an eyebrow, as though genuinely considering her observation, before leaning down so his forehead was almost resting against hers. "Guess I should probably try to curb that, huh? Little girls don't need to hear such bad words."

"I think I've heard and *said* my fair share," she replied,

giggling softly, her cheeks aching from how much she'd been smiling all morning.

His large hand cupped her chin, his thumb brushing against her as his dark eyes locked onto hers. The warmth in his gaze was inescapable, wrapping around her like a blanket, even more so as his cologne surrounded her senses, making her feel lightheaded in the best way.

"You better not curse, sunshine," he murmured in a husky timbre. "Little girls who say bad words get into trouble."

She swallowed hard, heat blooming in her chest and pooling low in her belly. Why did she get all squirmy every time he talked about punishing her? She'd been spanked before—sort of. During sex, anyway. But her previous Daddy had never actually punished her, and the thought of Storm doing so was both thrilling and terrifying.

Her thoughts scattered when his lips touched hers, gentle and fleeting but powerful enough to leave her breathless. When he pulled away, her heart was pounding so hard she thought he might actually hear it.

"Do you have any plans tonight?" he asked casually, his dark eyes still locked on hers.

She blinked, almost laughing at the question. "Uh, start a new book, maybe?"

Her words sounded pathetic even to her own ears, and for a moment, she was sure he'd realize how boring she was and regret offering to be her Daddy.

"Perfect," he said, his tone warm and decisive. "You can read while I make us dinner, and then we'll sit down and talk about what things are going to look like moving forward."

"You cook?" she blurted higher and louder than intended.

Storm chuckled, the sound deep and rich. "Yeah, baby. By cook, I mean I'll pull the containers out of the to-go bag and put the food on plates. Have a good day, and I'll pick you up at five."

He turned her gently, giving her bottom a firm swat that made her giggle and yelp as she scurried into her office. Her cheeks burned, and her bottom stung faintly through her skirt, but as she sat at her desk, the warmth radiating from the slight sting only made her smile even wider.

It was going to be a very good day.

# NINE
## STORM

"So, are you girls still mad at me?" Storm asked, a mix of curiosity and hesitation rumbling in his deep voice as he leaned casually against the back of a chair in the common room of the clubhouse.

At the table, Carlee, Ivy, and Remi looked up from their coloring books. He felt a small wave of relief when he didn't see any of them glaring at him.

"We weren't mad," Remi replied softly. "We were sad." She glanced at the others before continuing, "But we're not anymore. Our Daddies explained that it's okay for you to want a house of your own and that we'll still see you a lot. We thought maybe you wanted to move out of the clubhouse because you hated us."

Storm pulled out a chair and sat beside Ivy, with Carlee and Remi across from him. The weight of their words settled uncomfortably in his chest. He loathed that they'd ever thought that. Sure, he wasn't the type to wear his emotions on his sleeve, and his default setting was grumpy, but that didn't mean he didn't care about the Littles.

Reaching out, he ruffled Ivy's hair gently, her giggle relaxing the tension in the room. "I could never hate you," he said, his voice firm but kind. "You girls are the fucking highlight of my day."

"That's ten dollars in the swear jar," Carlee chimed in, raising her eyebrows like a disappointed schoolteacher.

Storm scowled, his brows knitting together. "Ten dollars? I thought it was five for the F-word."

Carlee shrugged, an impish grin spreading across her face. "Inflation's a bitch, isn't it?"

"Carlee!" he snapped. While he sounded exasperated, he was more playful than angry.

All three girls burst into giggles, their laughter filling the room. Grumbling under his breath, he reached into his pocket and handed over a ten-dollar bill. The Littles practically robbed him blind on a daily basis with their swear jar antics. Maybe it really was time to work on his cussing.

"As I was saying," he carried on, leveling them with a mock glare, "believe it or not, I love each and every one of you. I know I don't show it like some of the other guys, but I do. I'm not used to so much energy, though. I've always kept to myself, and when it was just us guys here, it was easy to do that. Having a house of my own will give me a place to go when I need a break. That doesn't mean I don't like you. Does that make sense?"

The girls nodded, their heads bobbing in unison. Ivy reached out to touch his arm, her small hand resting lightly on his forearm. "Just so you know," she said earnestly, "even though we're sometimes naughty and pull pranks on you, we love you, too. We're sorry if we kind of invaded your space. I guess you didn't really get a choice in that, huh?"

No, he hadn't. But looking at their wide eyes and genuine expressions, he couldn't bring himself to hold it against them. Besides, with Brook now in his life, he knew his brothers hadn't had much choice, either. Falling for Brook had been completely out of his control.

"No, I didn't get a choice," he admitted, his voice softening. "But that doesn't mean I wish things were different. You've all brightened our lives in ways you don't even realize. Everyone's different, though. I like my quiet time. I'm sorry if I ever made you upset." He looked at each of them in turn, holding their gazes to make sure they understood how much he meant it.

"We forgive you," Carlee declared dramatically, placing a hand over her heart. Then, her eyes sparkled with mischief. "Bet you're glad you've bought a house now so you can take Brook there and do wild things with her, huh?"

Storm chuckled, shaking his head. "We are *not* getting into a conversation about my sex life."

Carlee feigning innocence, scoffing. "I didn't say anything about your sex life, Stormy-Normy. I was simply talking about *other* things."

His glare was sharp but laced with humor. "Don't call me that, brat. And what 'other things' could you possibly be talking about?"

She shrugged, giggling as though she'd won some secret victory. "I don't know. But since you brought up sex… are you in love with Brook?"

Jesus Christ. Storm pinched the bridge of his nose, already regretting sitting down for this conversation. "You girls are impossible," he muttered, though the corners of his mouth twitched in reluctant amusement.

"Why are you asking about Storm's sex life, baby? Don't I keep you satisfied enough not to wonder about other people's private lives?" Atlas asked as he strode into the room, a teasing edge to his deep voice. His gaze settled on Carlee, who immediately turned scarlet.

The way Carlee's blush deepened made Storm laugh, a rare and genuine sound that rumbled from his chest. Carlee whipped her head toward him, narrowing her eyes and sticking out her tongue.

"Fucking Little girls," he said under his breath, shaking his head, though his smirk betrayed his fondness. Why had he ever wanted to get away from them?

The answer came screaming through the room as Harper bolted past, squealing at the top of her lungs, with Eden chasing her in a bear onesie. Storm sighed. *Right. That's why.* How was it possible for them to be so damn loud and chaotic *all* the time?

"You didn't answer the question," Remi quipped, her voice sweet yet pointed as she leaned forward to rest on her coloring book. "Are you in love with Brook? We really like her, and she looks at you like you're the most handsome man she's ever seen."

Storm froze for a second, caught off guard. "She does?"

Atlas scoffed, leaning against the door frame with a knowing grin. "Idiot. Even I see it."

Warmth flooded Storm's chest, unexpected and almost overwhelming. He sank back into his chair, letting the words settle. He knew he had strong feelings for Brook—feelings that scared him in their intensity—but he'd been unsure if she felt the same. They didn't know each other well yet, and he couldn't shake the doubt that his grumpy, brooding personality might push her away in the end.

"I like her," he admitted finally. "It's not that easy, though."

Ivy tipped her head to the side, her brows knitting in concern. "Why not?"

Storm let out a deep breath, staring at her for a moment, weighing up whether to share the mess of his past. The guys knew the baggage he carried from his ex, but he'd never told the girls the ins and outs of what happened. Maybe that was part of why they'd thought he disliked them—he'd always kept his distance.

"Because eventually, she's going to want someone better," he said gruffly. "Someone happier, less grumpy, less... moody. Someone who deserves her. She'll find someone like that, the same way my ex did."

Remi's little growl would've been intimidating if it weren't so adorable. It sounded more like a kitten hissing, and Storm couldn't help but crack a smile. "Fuck that bitch," Remi snapped, her tiny fist slamming on the table. "Your ex was a skanky bitch, faker than my glue-on eyelashes."

"Remi!" Atlas barked at his sister, his tone sharp, though his lips, fighting a laugh.

Remi shrugged, utterly unbothered. "What? I'm just telling the truth. I met Emmaline when you were together, and she was rude, whiny—*and not in a good way*—and she treated you like crap. She wasn't even Little. That was obvious to me, but you must've been blinded by her vagina or something."

"Remi!" Storm and Atlas shouted at the same time, though the other two girls dissolved into giggles.

Storm rubbed a hand over his face, shaking his head. He hadn't realized Remi knew that much about Emmaline. It had been years ago, back when Remi didn't spend nearly as much time at the clubhouse. Before she met her Daddy, Kade.

Carlee's voice broke through his thoughts. "Our point is, Brook is a true Little. She's not fake. And yeah, she's not grumpy like you, but she likes the quiet life, too. She hangs out with us, but she needs time to decompress, just like you do."

Ivy nodded in agreement. "And as much as you think women don't like your grumpy side, it's actually kind of hot. You may walk around scowling, acting all pissed off, but we know you have a good heart. What woman wouldn't want a guy who's an asshole to everyone else but soft for her?"

Storm groaned, holding out his hand. "Okay, that's it. Give me my money back. You brats have been cursing this entire conversation."

Carlee rolled her eyes dramatically but slapped the ten-dollar bill into his palm. "Don't change the subject, Stormy-Normy," Remi said, sounding rarely serious. "Love doesn't have to be hard. With the right person, it usually isn't. Don't let your shitty ex decide your future. You'll regret it if you don't take a chance with Brook."

Storm hated to admit it, but she was right. Deep down, he felt it—the pull toward Brook, the certainty that she was meant to be his. She was the missing piece he hadn't known he was searching for.

"Well," he leaned back in his chair, "you'll be thrilled to know that, for now, I *am* her Daddy."

The explosion of squeals and excited screams made his ears ring, but he couldn't help the smile that stretched across his face.

"I knew it would happen," Carlee said smugly.

He held up a hand to silence them. "We're taking it slow and seeing where things go."

There was only one problem with that plan: he didn't *want* to take it slowly. He wanted Brook in his bed every night. Hell, he wanted her in his life completely, and they hadn't even had sex yet. And the more he thought about it, the more Storm knew he'd never settle for anything less.

By the time Storm pulled up to Brook's workplace, the day had dragged endlessly, his mind a tangle of thoughts and his patience worn thin. After his conversation with the Littles earlier, he'd retreated to the shop, immersing himself in the meticulous task of inspecting Brook's car. The accident had left little more than a faint scratch on her bumper—nothing structural, nothing alarming—but he'd gone over every inch of it anyway. The other guy's car was likely just as unscathed, making an insurance claim probably unnecessary. Yet, even after ensuring her car's safety, a restless unease had settled in his chest, refusing to budge.

When he spotted Brook stepping outside alongside a coworker, it was as if a weight had lifted off his shoulders. The tightness in his muscles eased, replaced by a soothing contentment that rolled over him like a balm. He hadn't even realized how tense he'd been until the sight of her brought relief.

She waved goodbye to her coworker and skipped toward him—*skipped*. The lightness in her step sent a pang of warmth straight to his chest. Storm climbed out of his truck, rounding the hood to open the door for her. As she stopped in front of him, her cheeks flushed a delicate, rosy pink, and her gaze dropped shyly to the ground.

He tilted his head, studying her. *She's not used to being looked at like this, is she?* Openly. Directly. With every ounce of his focus.

"Hey, pretty girl," he murmured, his voice rougher than he intended as he reached out, pulling her gently into his chest. The moment she was there, he knew—she fit. Perfectly. She was made to be in his arms.

"Thanks for picking me up," she whispered, slipping her arms around his waist as she let out a soft sigh. The sound was so full of trust that it undid him a little. Did she feel the same sense of calm seeing him that he felt seeing her?

"Anytime, sunshine. Ready to go home? Atlas is bringing your car to your place later. It's good to go."

She lifted her head, her sparkling eyes locking onto his. Her lips—plump and glistening with cherry-scented gloss —curved into a smile, the sight teasing his senses and testing his restraint. His cock twitched as he stared, and he clenched his jaw. He'd never thought of himself as ruled by lust, but with Brook, everything was different. She unraveled him in ways he hadn't known were possible.

As she climbed into the truck, the curve of her ass stole his attention. He bit back a groan, his fingers spasming with the urge to touch her. *Goddamn, she's perfect.*

"Need to go anywhere before we head to your place?" he asked, sounding slightly strained as he slid into the driver's seat.

"Nope," she replied, a playful pop to the *P* before giggling softly.

Her lightness sent a jolt through him. She was in a playful mood, and it was downright adorable.

The drive to her apartment was mercifully short. As soon as they stepped into the entryway, Storm shut the door, locking it with a deliberate *click*. He couldn't wait another second. Pinning her gently against the wall, he captured her lips with his. The kiss was deep, hot, and all-consuming, the tension between them igniting like a spark to dry kindling. Her hands slid under his shirt, her fingers grazing the hard lines of his stomach.

"Brook," he muttered breathlessly against her lips, trying to steady himself. The last thing he wanted was for their first time to be a frantic tumble just inside her apartment door.

"Can we?" she asked, her voice soft but urgent, her gaze searching his. "Can we go to my bedroom? Please?"

Before he could respond, she tugged on his arm, leading him down the hall. Her room was an explosion of pastel colors, plush toys, and delicate touches that screamed *Little.* He barely registered any more details, his focus entirely on her—her flushed cheeks, her sparkling eyes, her lips still swollen from his kiss.

"We don't have to do this, sunshine," he said, steady but tender. He needed her to know she had an out, even if every fiber of his being begged her to want this as much as he did.

"I know," she replied, stepping closer. "But I want to. It doesn't have to be anything serious. I know we're seeing where things go, but I've been squirmy since this morning, and I might die if we don't do something."

Storm's brow arched, a smirk tugging at his lips. "You might die, baby? Don't you think that's a little dramatic?"

She shook her head with an adorably serious expression painted on her face. "Nu-uh. It could really happen. Death by arousal. And then you'd feel terrible because you could've kept me alive."

The playful defiance in her tone was a revelation. Beneath her sweetness was a brat just begging to be tamed. Storm's grin widened as he leaned in to whisper into her ear in a low rumble. "Well, baby, I can't have you dying on me, now, can I?"

From that moment on, there was no holding back. Storm knew—he was gone for her. Completely. *Forever.*

She shook her head. "Nope. That would be bad luck."

This sassy side of her was so fucking cute.

"Do you know what a safeword is?" he asked.

"Yes. I don't have one, but I know the stop light system."

That pleased the hell out of him. He hoped that meant

any partners she'd had in the past had at least been good men.

"Good girl. So you'll say red if you want everything to stop?"

"Yes."

He took a step toward her, reaching out to lift her chin.

"Yes, Daddy."

A dimple appeared as she smiled widely. How he hadn't noticed it before, he had no idea.

"Yes, Daddy."

His cock ached, and he regretted not masturbating before he'd picked her up because the likelihood of him lasting long was slim. He'd make it up to her, though.

When he kissed her this time, it was demanding and wild, their hands roaming each other's bodies desperately. She was soft and curvy beneath his touch. When he cupped her ass and squeezed, she moaned, and he nearly came right then and there.

"Fuck, sunshine. You're killing me," he ground out.

Her only response was a whimper as she bit down on her bottom lip.

"Arms up." As soon as she obeyed, he lifted her top up and over her head, letting it drop to the floor as he moved on to her skirt.

At the same time, she yanked off his T-shirt and ran her fingers over the lines of his tattoos. A trail of goosebumps rose on his skin, chasing her fingers. There was no doubt in his mind that things would never be the same after he had her. She would be his, and he would be hers.

*Fuck seeing where it goes.*

Her breath hitched when he unsnapped her bra. She

tried to cover her heavy breasts, but he grabbed hold of her arms before she could. Why the fuck she was trying to hide he had no idea, but that was going to be a rule.

"Keep your arms at your sides. I want to play with and suck on these pretty tits for a bit, sunshine."

She whimpered and nodded, and when she slid her fingers through his hair, gripping it tightly, he groaned. Her nipples were hard peaks, practically begging for his mouth, and as soon as he latched on to one, she moaned and arched up for him even more. So full and plush, he wanted to spend hours on her beautiful breasts.

Flicking his tongue over one, he rolled the other between his fingers, loving all the sounds she was making for him. Storm liked being in control, but it seemed like around her, he couldn't manage very much over himself.

"Storm," she cried out when he bit down on her nipple.

He lifted his head, his heart hammering and his cock throbbing. She drove him wild, and they hadn't even fucked yet.

"Call me Storm one more time and I'm taking my belt to your ass, sunshine. I'm Daddy to you now."

Her gaze flicked down to his, and he resumed sucking her tits while keeping his eyes locked on hers so she could see the gravity of his statement. He might not have any control when it came to her, but that didn't mean he wouldn't punish her.

"Oh my God. That feels so good," she whined, lifting her hips to meet his.

They ground against each other like a couple of needy animals, but he didn't care. It felt too fucking good. If all he could do for the rest of his life was dry hump Brook, he'd fucking settle for that. Hell, he was pretty sure he'd settle for just about anything so long as it was with her.

No one had had ever made him think about rings, vows, and a happily ever after before, but those thoughts were quickly becoming a permanent fixture in his mind.

"You taste so fucking good, baby girl. I bet your pussy tastes even better. Are you going to be a good girl and cream all over my tongue for me?"

Something flashed across her face that had him pausing immediately. Almost like she was frightened or worried. He didn't like that.

"What's wrong, Brook?"

She shook her head. "You...um, you don't have to do that. I don't need oral."

Raising his eyebrows, he lifted his head and pinned her with a stern look. "And why the fuck not? I want to. I want to lick, fuck, and taste every fucking hole you have, and I plan to, sunshine. So tell me, why the fuck do you look like I just told you something terrible?"

# TEN
## BROOK

Well, shoot.

Now she'd gone and ruined the moment.

And Storm looked pissed.

How was she supposed to tell him that he shouldn't go down on her because she didn't taste good? The last thing she wanted was for him to do it and discover how bad it was and then decide he didn't want to be her Daddy. At least she was doing the polite thing and warning him. He should thank her for it instead of being so cranky.

"Sunshine, look at me," he snapped sharply, pulling her out of her spiraling thoughts.

When she obeyed, she pulled her bottom lip between her teeth, suddenly regretting asking for him to take her to her bedroom. Why did she have to be such a needy, sex-starved woman?

"Did someone say something mean about your pussy?"

She wasn't sure that she liked how intuitive he seemed to be about her. Was she that obvious?

"My ex, um, he said that girls my size shouldn't expect oral because no man would want to have his head between jiggly thighs."

The hand he had resting on her hip tightened so much that she winced, but he didn't seem to notice. Instead, he stared at her, and she could swear storm clouds came together over his head with loud thunder and strikes of lightning getting ready to explode. He looked so intense that Brook thought her knees may give way.

"It's really okay," she said hurriedly. "I don't need oral. We can have sex, or I could suck you off." She made her voice light at the end of the sentence.

Storm slid a hand from her breast to her neck, wrapping his large hand around it and squeezing firmly on the sides of her throat. The sensation sent a rush of arousal through her. Huh. That was new.

"Your ex was a fucking loser, sunshine. The only kind of fucking thighs I want my head between are the jiggly kind. The kind that are full and thick and have imperfections. The kind that brings me to my fucking knees because of how beautiful and delicious they are. And baby, I plan on having my face between yours a whole fucking lot because I like it. And your thighs, they're quickly becoming my fucking favorite."

Every ounce of air rushed from her lungs as she stared up at him, unsure how to respond. She wasn't sure she could even speak if she wanted to.

"You're going to learn very fucking quickly how obsessed I am with your body, Brook. I've stroked my cock multiple times a day since I met you while thinking about all the nasty fucked-up things I want to do to you. So whatever thoughts that asshole put into your head, I need you to forget about them right fucking now. You're perfect. Beautiful. Thick. Delicious. Sweet. All the fucking things I don't deserve, but I'm too selfish to walk away from."

And then, without waiting for her response, he moved down her body, yanking her panties off so forcefully she heard the sure sound of fabric ripping. Her legs hit the side of the bed, and Storm pushed her gently. As soon as she lay down, his mouth was on her clit instantly. Without giving her time to think, he started sucking on the delicate nub, she nearly catapulted off the bed.

Whoa. She'd never experienced that sort of sensation before. Her vision blurred, and the words came out as mumbling that couldn't be made out, but Storm didn't seem to care. He was too busy licking and sucking on her pussy like it was his last meal, and it felt too dang good to question if she tasted good or if he was enjoying it. His enthusiasm alone told her he was.

"Daddy!" she cried as her body tightened and her legs started to shake.

"Come on my face, sunshine. Give me all your cream," he commanded while playing with her.

When he slid a finger into her and curled it, she screamed and thrashed. She fisted the frilly bedding and tilted her head back, crying out over and over, her pussy pulsing as he continued to eat her out through her orgasm.

As soon as Storm pulled away, he stood with purpose, his hands moving to unbuckle his belt. The clink of the metal echoed in the quiet room, a sound that sent a shiver down Brook's spine. What was it about the sound of a man's belt that was so damn hot? Her heart thudded as he shifted to the button of his jeans, popping it open with ease. Every movement was unhurried, confident, and utterly mesmerizing.

When he kicked off his boots and stepped out of his pants, her breath hitched. Her gaze roamed over him, drinking in the sight of his muscular, tattooed figure. His body was a canvas, the intricate ink adding to his rugged allure. But it was the outline of his cock, enormous and rigid against his briefs, that made her pulse race. Her mind swirled with anticipation and just a hint of nervousness. How was *that* going to fit inside her?

"Still want to keep going, sunshine?" he asked, low and rough, a rumble that sent a thrill straight through her core.

She met his gaze, her wide eyes locking onto his.

"Yes, Daddy." Brook was trembling with need, which made her whisper quiver.

Oh, yes, she wanted this. She wanted *him*. She wasn't exaggerating when she'd said she might die if they didn't do this. They hadn't known each other for long, but every moment with him was natural and undeniable. From the first time they'd met, the connection had been obvious. She wasn't sure she was good at relationships, but for Storm, she was willing to try.

Storm pulled a condom from his wallet, the deliberate movement making her body buzz with anticipation. After tossing the wallet onto the pile of their discarded clothes, he ripped the wrapper open, the crinkle of foil loud in the stillness. The only other sound in the room was their shared, shallow, rapid breathing.

"After this, we're going to talk about your rules and where this is going, sunshine," he said, his tone firm yet full of tenderness. His index finger moved between them, emphasizing his point. "Because once I've had my cock in your pussy, I'm not 'seeing where this goes.' You're mine, and I'm yours. That's final. Do you have a problem with that?"

She shook her head quickly, her throat tight with emotion and desire.

"Words, Brook. Use your words for Daddy."

Her heart flipped at the title.

"No, Daddy," she words were soft but clear, "I don't have a problem with that."

Satisfied, Storm rolled the condom on with practiced ease, then knelt on the mattress between her legs. His broad shoulders and stern presence made her feel small and safe. He bracketed her head with his forearms, his body hovering over her like a shield. The head of his cock brushed against her clit, sparking a jolt of pleasure that had her hips bucking instinctively.

"So needy, baby," he murmured with a low chuckle, his voice tinged with admiration. "I fucking love that, but I don't want to go too fast and hurt you."

Her hands slid around his neck, her fingers tangling in his hair as she gazed up at him. His dark eyes, usually so intense and guarded, were more tender now. He kept showing her sides of himself that she hadn't expected—gentleness, patience, a quiet vulnerability that made her fall for him a little more each second.

Was it too soon to call it love? That four-letter word she'd never thought she'd feel with a man? Maybe. But right then and there, it didn't matter to Brook.

"You won't hurt me," she whispered, sounding sure of herself despite the whirl of emotions swirling inside.

His gaze never wavered, piercing hers with a depth that left her breathless. "Never, baby. I'll always protect you."

And Brook believed him. Storm was many things— gruff, commanding, sometimes a little too intense—but above all else, he was a protector. That much she knew without a shadow of a doubt.

Slowly, Storm shifted his hips forward, his movements careful and deliberate. The warmth of his skin against her thighs was intoxicating. As the head of his cock slid between her slick folds, a soft, unmistakable sound filled the air—her arousal.

Oh, God. That was *mortifying*.

"Fuck," he groaned with clear approval. "That's a beautiful sound. Love that you're so turned on for me, sunshine."

Her blush deepened, but her body answered on its own, arching toward him in a silent plea for more. In that moment, there was nothing else—just them, just this, and the fire building between them.

Okay, maybe she didn't need to be embarrassed. Obviously, he liked it.

Brook didn't have time to ponder it because she was suddenly stretched almost to the point of pain. He was so thick, and it had been a long time since she'd been with anyone.

"Sorry, sweet girl. Fuck, I don't like that pain in your eyes," he gritted out as he stilled.

"I'm okay. I just need a second to adjust," she replied breathlessly.

Storm was the kind of man who would blame himself for her discomfort and that wasn't what she wanted. After all, the man couldn't help that he had a huge cock.

He didn't move for a long few seconds until she started wiggling against him, desperate for more.

"Keep going, Daddy."

That made his lips twitch. "Are you trying to boss me around? That's not how this works, Little one."

She giggled, loving this light, playful side of him. There was no doubt that he would call the shots and be strict with her, but she liked that he wasn't serious all the time. She also liked that it was a side he didn't show to everyone.

"Yes, Daddy. I'm the boss. Now, fuck me."

His eyebrows shot up, and before she knew what was happening, he pulled out of her, flipped her onto her stomach, and started peppering her bottom with spanks.

They were sharp and fast but not really painful. Instead, with each one, her pussy grew wetter and her body hotter.

"Ouchie!" she cried out without any real force.

"Want to share with me again who the boss is, sunshine?" he asked, pausing the spanking.

She twisted her head so she could peek back at him, his hard cock bobbing against his muscular stomach as he hovered over her.

"It's me, Daddy. I'm the boss. And if you don't fuck me soon, I might have to take matters into my own hands."

He froze, his surprise obvious as he stared down at her.

"Jesus, when did you get so sassy? And here, I thought you were a good Little girl, but I show you my dick one time and you get mouthy."

She burst out laughing as he started spanking her again. They were being silly, and laughing during sex was probably weird, but it felt perfect with Storm.

"Okay, I'll be good," she moaned when he slid his fingers between her thighs. "I'm sorry. Please don't stop."

"Oh, *now* you're sorry," he teased. "Who's the boss, sunshine?"

She whimpered as he grabbed her hips and pulled her up, her hot ass meeting his hips, his cock rubbing against her clit.

"You are." She tried to grind against him, and thankfully, he let her get away with it for a second before he slipped the head of his cock into her tight opening.

"Yeah, baby, I'm the boss," he muttered. "And you're the fucking queen, so don't ever forget that."

Her heart pounded, and she pushed back on him again, biting her lip to keep from wincing. He took it slow, and it felt as though it took forever before he was fully seated inside her.

"You okay, baby?"

"Yes, Daddy," she whispered, her pussy clenching around him.

He held onto her, his hands gripping her hips as he slowly slid out and then back in. It didn't take long before she was moving along with him and groaning into the mattress.

"I'm not going to last long. You're so goddamn tight," he ground out.

The fact he was struggling to keep his composure was so damn hot. It made her feel powerful and sexy, knowing he was as turned on as she was because she definitely wasn't going to last very long, either.

Storm slid one of his hands up her back and buried his fingers in her hair, fisting her tresses firmly and tugging as he fucked her harder and faster. Both of them moaned and cried out their pleasure as their orgasms built.

When he let go of one of her hips and reached around to rub her clit, she screamed, every muscle in her body tensing. The room turned blurry as his thrusts became erratic and wild. He was close, but she was closer.

"Daddy!" she keened.

"Yeah, baby, come for me. Come all over my dick."

His command was met with obedience as she exploded around him, her body trembling violently while her pussy clamped down on him like a vise.

"Ugh, fuck!" he shouted, his cock throbbing inside her as he came at the same time.

They stayed like that for a minute or two until she couldn't hold herself up any longer and collapsed onto the soft bedding. He chuckled softly and rubbed her back, then he got up from the bed and walked his perfect, naked ass to the bathroom.

She'd heard that sex could be life changing, but she'd never actually believed it until now because she was definitely a new woman.

"How old is your Little?" Storm asked, his voice low and warm, the deep timbre rumbling through his chest like distant thunder.

Brook nuzzled closer, her cheek pressed against his solid, warm chest, enjoying the rhythmic rise and fall of his breathing. Her body still hummed from the euphoria he'd pulled her into, leaving her blissfully relaxed yet unguarded. Vulnerable, even. She hesitated for a beat, her fingers tracing absent patterns on his tattooed skin, before answering in a voice soft and slightly muffled against him.

"I think I fall around two or three," she admitted, her cheeks heating as the words slipped out. It felt strange saying it out loud, even though she'd thought about it plenty of times. This was the first time she'd said it with such certainty. The only reason she managed it now was the comfort of knowing that Carlee and some of the other Littles fell into the same range. Surely, Storm was used to it. Right?

"That's a good age, sunshine," he murmured, his large hand lazily stroking her back in long, soothing motions. "Just sweet enough to have me wrapped around your cute little finger but old enough to still be a brat and earn spankings."

Her lips quirked into a smile she couldn't manage to hide. Thank God they were snuggled so close, she thought. At least he couldn't see her face. Somehow, whenever Storm talked about spanking her, it sent a thrill racing through her that she didn't entirely know what to do with. Her cheeks flushed hotter, her skin tingling with an excitement that made her toes curl and her stomach flip.

"Have you ever been spanked, Brook?" His tone turned teasing, though his curiosity seemed genuine. "You get squirmy whenever I bring it up."

*Crap.* How could he read her so easily, even when he wasn't looking at her? His ability to see right through her was both thrilling and unnerving.

"Um, not really," she stammered, her voice wobbling slightly. "I mean, not like how Carlee gets spanked. During sex, I have." Her heart raced as the confession spilled from her, and she bit her lip to keep from babbling.

Storm chuckled softly, the sound vibrating through his chest and into her. It wasn't mocking, but rather a warm, low rumble that made her comforted and a little flustered. His thumb continued to brush over her bare arm in lazy circles, the simple touch grounding her in the moment. Being tucked into him like this gave her a sense of security she hadn't even realized she'd been missing.

"Well," he drawled, his voice dropping slightly, darker now, "I can promise you this, baby. The spanking you got while we were fucking is *nothing* compared to the spanking you'll get for being naughty."

Her breath hitched, but not from fear. Storm didn't scare her. On the contrary, she'd never felt safer in her life. The way he spoke, the way he touched her—it wasn't just physical. He gave her a sense of being cherished. Protected. He might play with her and push her limits, but there wasn't a single part of her that doubted he'd take care of her, even at her most vulnerable.

"Tell me about your asshole ex," he said after a pause, softening his words slightly, but they still held that commanding edge. "Was he your Daddy?"

Brook blinked, surprised by the shift in tone. Storm wasn't one for long conversations, but tonight felt different —like he wanted to understand her on a deeper level. Despite the turn toward an uncomfortable topic, she found herself wanting to answer. Wanting to let him in. Let him know who she was.

"He was. Sort of," she admitted hesitantly. Her fingers fidgeted with the edge of the blanket draped over them both. "It was more of a play thing for him."

Storm's arm tightened around her, his grip firm but not harsh, like he was anchoring her to him. He didn't reply immediately, and the silence stretched just long enough for her to glance up at him.

His dark eyes locked onto hers, unwavering and intense. "I need you to understand something, sunshine," he said with each word steady and weighted with meaning. "Nothing about this will be a 'play thing' for me. This is serious. We are serious. Our dynamic will be real—not something casual you can dip into when it's convenient."

Her heart thudded in her chest at the conviction apparent in his tone. She could see the sincerity in his eyes, the way he held her gaze like he needed her to truly hear him. And she did. Every word settled over her like a promise, steadfast and unyielding.

Her lips parted slightly, her breath catching at the weight of his words.

"You'll have rules, boundaries, and consequences," he continued, his voice firm but not unkind. "I'll take care of you, discipline you when you need it, spoil you, and treat you like the princess you are. But if you're expecting this to be some casual, on-and-off thing, you're wrong. I don't do casual, and I sure as fuck don't play when it comes to being a Daddy."

Brook's chest tightened, her emotions swirling in a mix of awe, excitement, and a hint of fear—not of him, but of the enormity of what he was offering. He wasn't just offering to be her Daddy; he was offering to be her *everything*.

"I understand," she whispered with a slight tremble but steady with certainty. "I want that. I want *you*."

The flicker of relief in his expression was subtle yet unmistakable. A vulnerable side to him she hadn't seen. He leaned down, pressing a gentle kiss to her forehead. "Good," he said simply, pulling her close again. "Because you're mine now, sunshine. And I don't half-ass anything when it comes to the people I care about."

She melted into him, her heart thudding as his words settled deep into her soul. For the first time in a long time, she was exactly where she was meant to be.

His words settled in her chest like a weighted blanket, wrapping her in a sincere, reassuring warmth she hadn't realized she craved so deeply.

"When was the last time you had a Little?" Brook asked softly, her voice hesitant as she traced the tip of her finger over one of his muscular pecs.

Storm swallowed, his dark eyes fixed on her with an intensity that made her heart skip. For a fleeting moment, something unspoken flickered in his gaze that told her she wasn't going to like the answer. Before he got the chance to speak, her phone rang, interrupting the intimate moment.

She startled, rolling to grab her bag from the floor next to the bed. Normally, she would've ignored it, but she'd talked to her mom earlier in the day and found out she had the flu. Brook had made her mom promise to call if she needed anything. Without checking the screen, she swiped to answer.

"Hello?" she said, pressing the phone to her ear.

Silence greeted her on the other end of the line.

"Hello?" she repeated, her brows furrowing. Pulling the phone away, she glanced at the screen.

*Unknown number.*

"Hello?" she tried once more.

The call abruptly ended with a sharp *beep*. She sighed, her shoulders sagging as she tossed the phone onto the end of the bed.

"Who was that?" Storm's deep voice cut through the room, his tone sharper now as he sat up, his brows pinched with a scowl.

She shook her head, brushing off the unease settling in her gut. "I'm not sure. Probably a wrong number."

But the truth lingered at the edges of her mind, nagging. It was the second time today she'd received a call like that.

Storm rose from the bed, pulling on his boxer briefs, then his jeans and T-shirt. Brook suddenly felt acutely aware of her nakedness, her cheeks heating as she wrapped a soft throw blanket around her. Moving to her light pink dresser, she started rifling through it for something to wear.

"What do you think you're doing, sunshine?" Storm's growl stopped her in her tracks, and she turned toward him, biting back a smile. His grouchy demeanor didn't faze her anymore; she'd come to realize his bark was much worse than his bite.

"I'm putting on some clothes," she replied, trying to sound matter-of-fact.

"No, baby." His voice dropped, a commanding edge slipping into it. "It's my job to pick your clothes and dress you now. You can choose what you wear to work, but when we're at home, that's all on me. Do you have special clothes for your Little, or should I just pick something I like?"

A rush of butterflies erupted in her stomach, her heart fluttering as she pointed toward the closet. "The left side of the closet and this dresser... that's my Little wardrobe."

Without hesitation, Storm began sifting through her clothes. When he pulled out a pair of high-waisted cotton panties with scalloped edges and tiny pink hearts, her cheeks burned hotter.

*This is really happening.*

Her ex had barely scratched the surface of what being a Daddy meant, but Storm? Storm was already showing her what care and attention truly looked like.

"In our dynamic, our relationship," he said, calm but firm as he continued sorting through her wardrobe, "your safeword will always be red. It isn't just for when we're having sex—it's for anything. Any time, in *any* situation."

Brook blinked at him, the gravity of his words sinking in.

"You wouldn't get mad?" she asked hesitantly.

Storm froze, turning to look at her with a scowl that would've sent lesser men running. "Did your ex get mad if you used your safeword?" he asked, his tone sharp with disbelief.

She shrugged, lowering her gaze. "He didn't like the idea of safewords. He said I shouldn't need one if I trusted him..." She trailed off.

"Jesus Christ, sunshine." His voice was a deep growl as he stalked over to her, his towering presence both protective and imposing. "Who was this fucker?"

Brook shrank slightly, the intensity of his reaction catching her off guard. But when he cupped her chin and tilted her head to meet his gaze, she saw nothing but genuine concern etched into his face.

"I don't care if you trust me with your life," he said deliberately. "A safeword should always be there. It's not about trust—it's about safety. I would *never* be upset if you used it. It's there for a reason—to protect you, to keep you safe and healthy. I'm human, baby, and I'm not perfect. Things that feel fine one day might not feel like that the next, which is normal. Do you understand?"

A lump formed in her throat as she nodded. "Yes," she whispered, her voice barely audible.

"Good," he said softly, brushing a thumb over her cheek. "Because in this dynamic, your safety and happiness come first. Always."

Her chest tightened with emotion, and as he pulled her into his arms, the last remnants of doubt dissolved. For the first time in her life, she felt truly seen, valued, and cherished. And more now than ever before, she believed this wasn't something fleeting—it was the beginning of something lasting, something *real*.

How was it possible for her to feel so emotional over a man she barely knew? The thought twisted inside her, confusing and exhilarating at the same time. Maybe it was because every time she turned around, Storm did something unexpected. He wasn't just the gruff, brooding man he appeared to be. There was so much more to him—a complexity that intrigued and unsettled her. It made her chest ache to think of all the people who might have judged Storm without taking the time to see the man beneath the tough exterior.

"Red is the universal safeword in the club, too," Storm said. "So, if at any time, one of my brothers says or does something you don't like, you say red, and they'll stop immediately. We all kind of look out for each other's Littles without realizing it sometimes, but I know some of the girls don't feel comfortable with anyone but their Daddy. We'll talk more about that later."

As he spoke, he held up a light-pink sweater in front of her, the delicate fabric contrasting with his rugged hands. "Arms up."

"I need a bra," she replied barely above a whisper.

His eyebrows pinched slightly as he glanced between the sweater and her. "Why? We're not going anywhere tonight."

Heat flared across her skin, and she motioned toward her chest awkwardly. "My breasts are too big to just… hang free."

A slow, wicked smile spread across his face, making her knees feel like jelly. "No, baby. They're just fucking perfect, and it's not healthy to have them strapped up in a bra all the time. When we're alone, you won't wear a bra. I'll allow one when we're around other people or when you're at work. Now, arms up, don't make me repeat myself."

Her heart pounded as she slowly lifted her arms, letting the blanket she'd wrapped around herself slip to the floor. The moment she remembered she was completely naked, she instinctively moved to cover as much of her body as she could, but Storm was faster. His strong hands gently but firmly catching her wrists.

"Rule number one," he said, firm but not unkind, "no hiding from Daddy. When you're undressed, you don't try to cover yourself. I want to see my sunshine. Understand?"

She bit her bottom lip, her cheeks flaming as she nodded. His hands guided her arms upward again, and he dropped the sweater over her head. The soft fabric slid down her skin, covering her just enough to feel modest but still leaving her vulnerable under his intense gaze.

It was going to take time to adjust to his demands. Since she'd been her own caretaker for so long, her rules had been minimal, and there had been no one to enforce them. But now, with Storm, things were going to be very different.

"We're going to talk more about your rules and limits over dinner," he said slightly softer this time. "For now, I want to get you dressed, and I want you to spend some time in Little Space."

Storm knelt in front of her, holding out the pair of high-waisted cotton panties he'd gotten out of her dresser. The sight of them made her blush, but she stepped into them without hesitation. As he pulled them up her legs and settled them on her hips, she let out a deep breath. The snug, comfortable fit, tiny pink hearts, and scalloped edges seemed to invite her Little side forward, like it was being coaxed out gently.

"Come on, baby," Storm said, holding out his hand.

She hesitated, glancing around for a pair of bottoms. "I need pants."

"No, you don't," he replied, his voice firm but warm. "You're going to spend a lot of time like this when we're alone. Little girls don't need a bunch of clothes on when they're home and comfy."

Her cheeks burned, but the way his large hand wrapped around hers made her feel safe, like she could let go of the reins for once, something she was desperate for. He led her into the living room with a quiet confidence that made it seem like he'd been in her apartment a hundred times before. His natural ease was something she admired, and it helped her relax. It felt like she could truly let her guard down with him.

"Do you have any toys?" he asked casually.

The question caught her off guard, and her cheeks flamed even brighter. "Yes. I have some."

There was no point in being bashful or hiding this side of herself. Storm was around the other Littles regularly, so she suspected nothing would surprise him.

"Show me."

Swallowing thickly, Brook led him to the eight-cubby shelf she also used as a TV stand and pulled open one of the drawers then moved to the next. Each cube had different kinds of toys.

"You like Barbies, I see," he said as he ran his hand over the small of her back.

A shiver ran through her, and she was overly aware that while he was fully dressed, she was in not very much clothing. It was another thing that made her feel Little.

Brook glanced up at him, her eyes searching his face for any sign of judgment, but there was none. Instead, Storm's lips curved into a soft, knowing smile, the kind that made her stomach flutter.

"Barbies were my favorite growing up," she admitted quietly. "I guess I never really let them go."

Storm crouched slightly to get a better look at the neatly arranged dolls in their miniature outfits and plastic heels. "You've got quite the collection. Do you play with them often?"

Her fingers fidgeted with the hem of her sweater that barely grazed her thighs. "Yeah. When I need to decompress, they are my go-to other than coloring. Oh, and reading, of course."

He straightened, his towering frame effortlessly commanding the space without a trace of intimidation. "That's good," he said simply, like it was the most natural thing in the world. "We all need an outlet."

The ease in his tone made her cheeks cool slightly, the embarrassment fading into something more gentle. She glanced at him again, watching as his eyes scanned the rest of her cubbies. There was something about the way he looked—curious but never intrusive—that made her want to open up to him more.

"You want to see my favorite?" she asked, surprising herself.

He gave her a nod. "Only if you want to show me."

Brook turned back to the cubby, reaching into one of the drawers to pull out a doll with long, flowing auburn hair and a sparkling purple dress. The paint on the doll's face was slightly faded, and the edges of her dress were fraying, but it was the one she'd had the longest.

"This is Lily," Brook said, holding the doll delicately. "I've had her since I was a kid. We've been through a lot together."

Storm took a step closer, his gaze softening as he looked at the doll. "Lily's seen some adventures, huh?"

Brook nodded and giggled softly. "Oh, yeah."

Storm's smile widened, and for a moment, it felt like he wasn't just looking at the doll—he was looking at her, really *seeing* her. "Why don't you play with Lily and the other dolls while I order dinner? Does Italian sound okay? Anything you don't like or are allergic to?"

"No vegetables."

That made him laugh, and when he wrapped his hand around her hair and tugged her head back to kiss her, she went breathless. "Nice try, sunshine. You're having vegetables with dinner."

Well, that just sucked.

"Baby, put your toys away and come eat."

Brook glanced up from where she was lying tummy down on the floor with her feet swaying in the air. Storm had mostly left her alone for the past hour, only interrupting her playtime to set a sippy cup of water near her and to pat her bottom a few times. It was as if he knew she needed some time to herself but also wanted her to know he was there for her.

He'd made himself comfortable on the couch and turned on a football game, watching it in his own comfortable silence. Some people might have found it strange that they were both doing their own thing in the same room, but it felt totally normal to her.

Frowning, she sat up on her knees and gathered her dolls. "Can I play with them again after we eat?"

Without hesitating, he shook his head. "Not tonight, baby. After dinner, I'm giving you a bath, and then we're going to talk for a while before I put you to bed."

Letting out a dramatic sigh, she stood and dropped her Barbies in their allotted cube.

"Keep sighing like that, and you can eat dinner with a hot bottom, sunshine. Giving me attitude isn't going to work in your favor."

*Sheesh.*

Her bottom clenched, and she quickly wiped the glare off her face before she moved to the small dining table where he'd set out their plates.

"I wasn't having an attitude, Daddy."

She was *totally* having an attitude, but she'd keep that to herself. She wasn't sure she was ready to go over her Daddy's knee quite yet.

# ELEVEN
## STORM

S torm couldn't help the small, satisfied grin that tugged at his lips as he watched her carefully. He liked seeing her naughty side—loved it, actually. It showed her trust in him; that she wasn't afraid to test his boundaries or show her true self. And she shouldn't be afraid. Not of him.

Storm might be a grumpy bastard, and he'd definitely be a strict Daddy when needed, but he would always make sure Brook had a safe space to be Little. To let her wild, playful side be alive and free without fear of judgment. He'd enjoy reining her back in when the time came, too. It was only a matter of time before she found herself over his knee; after all, Littles couldn't help themselves.

Even though he could see the reluctance flickering across her face, she set her Barbies aside, neatly placing them in their designated cubby. She padded over to the table, her feet dragging slightly, and sat down when he pulled out a chair for her. He pushed her in with a firm but gentle motion, leaning down to press a quick kiss to the crown of her head. The simple act made her cheeks flush, filling him with a sense of pride and possessiveness that he couldn't quite put into words.

Settling into his seat beside her, he kept both plates in front of him, ignoring the questioning glance she shot his way. Without a word, he picked up his fork and scooped up some of the creamy pasta. Feeding her was something she hadn't wanted last time, but things were different now. He was her Daddy, and taking care of her in every way was part of his role. It wasn't just about discipline—it was about nurturing her, spoiling her, and making sure she was cherished.

"Open, sunshine," he said softly.

Her gaze met his, wide and sparkling, and after a moment's hesitation, she obeyed, parting her lips. He slipped the fork into her mouth, watching her cheeks turn a delicate shade of pink as she tasted the pasta. Between her bites, he took some of the food for himself, enjoying the quiet intimacy of the moment. It felt so natural and right to care for her like this.

"Do you only use sippy cups, or do you use bottles, too?" he asked after a few bites.

Her reaction was immediate. A deep blush spread over her cheeks, and she ducked her head, her lashes fluttering as she fidgeted with the hem of her sweater. "I only have sippy cups," she murmured, her voice barely above a whisper.

That wasn't exactly a full answer, and Storm's brow arched slightly as he observed her. "Have you ever used a bottle or thought about using one?"

He kept his gaze fixed on her, wanting to catch any flicker of expression that crossed her face.

"I've thought about it," she admitted so softly that he almost didn't catch it. "I've never tried one, though."

His chest tightened. Storm reached out, his fingers brushing her cheek as he offered her a small smile. "We'll add that to our list of things to try."

Her eyes widened slightly, and she bit her lip, but she nodded. The vulnerability in her expression tugged at something deep within him, solidifying what he already knew—he wanted to give her *everything*. Every comfort, every joy, and every ounce of safety she needed to truly thrive as his Little girl.

Reaching across to her, Storm wrapped his fingers around her wrist, bringing her hand to his mouth kiss her palm.

"'Kay. Thank you, Daddy."

Something settled inside of him. Making Brook happy was quickly becoming addictive. Seeing her smile was everything. It softened something in him that he hadn't realized had gone hard. Maybe it had happened after Emmaline, he wasn't sure. This sweet girl in front of him was changing it, though, and he liked it.

"I want to take you to the house I'm buying," Storm said suddenly, breaking the comfortable silence that had settled between them.

Brook looked up, her eyes curious and bright. She tilted her head slightly, chewing a bite of pasta as she processed his words. It wasn't just an invitation—it felt like more, like he was sharing a piece of himself with her. And for some reason, it was important to him that she see it before everything was finalized. Her apartment was fine—cozy, safe, and practical—but the thought of her in his house stirred something deep inside his chest. He was already thinking about the future, about making her a permanent part of his life, and he wanted her to love the place as much as he did.

After she swallowed, she smiled softly. "I've already seen the house. I work in the real estate office, remember?"

The corners of his mouth twitched into a subtle smirk. Of course she'd already seen it. It was her job. He should've guessed.

"It's beautiful," she continued. "One of my favorite listings recently. I was kind of surprised you went for that one."

Her words warmed him in a way he hadn't expected. Yeah, he'd been surprised, too. The house wasn't the kind of place he'd ever envisioned for himself, but the moment he had stepped inside, it felt right. He could already imagine Brook playing in the big backyard, hosting her friends for Little gatherings. He could picture summer BBQs, stringing up Christmas lights, and having their moms over for dinner.

Storm had never thought of himself as the traditional type of guy, but with Brook, everything felt different. He wanted to give her a stable, comfortable home where she could be herself, where she could thrive and make it her own. Knowing the house had been one of her favorites reassured him that he was making the right decision.

His life had revolved around motorcycles for so long, but now Brook was quickly becoming his primary focus.

She was the calm in his chaos, the warmth he hadn't realized he needed.

It was probably too soon to ask her to move in with him once he got the keys—hell, he didn't even have them yet. That was a next-week problem. He still had seven days before closing, plenty of time to figure out how to broach the subject with her.

Storm scooped up another bite of pasta and held it out for Brook, watching as she obediently opened her mouth. He offered her sips from her sippy cup between bites, feeling an odd sense of satisfaction in the simple act of taking care of her. She trusted him, and that was something he didn't take lightly.

"Do you use a pacifier?" he asked.

Brook's cheeks turned pink, and she hesitated for a moment before nodding slowly. "Yes. Usually when I'm reading or going to bed."

His cock twitched at her shy admission. Fuck, he liked that. She was so naturally Little, so sweet and innocent in a way that tugged at every protective instinct he had. Perfect for him. Unlike his ex, who had balked at the idea of even trying a sippy cup, Brook embraced it. She didn't have to try—it was simply who she was.

When they finished eating, Storm took their plates to the kitchen and rinsed them before loading them into the dishwasher. Brook came up behind him, wanting to help, but he waved her off.

"Good girl for eating your vegetables without a fight," he praised.

She giggled softly, a sound that wrapped around his

heart like a ribbon. "I figured I didn't have much of a choice. They weren't terrible, though."

Storm smirked and took her hand, guiding her toward the bathroom. "You had a choice, baby. But if you'd chosen to battle me, I would've thrown them in a blender and fed them to you that way. Daddy will get nutrients into you one way or the other. Or, as a last resort, Doc can help me administer them into your bottom."

Her eyes widened in shock, and her mouth fell open with disbelief. He could tell she wasn't used to having a Daddy like him—someone firm but playful, someone who genuinely cared about her well-being. Hell, her ex hadn't been a real Daddy at all. Storm planned to change that. He'd show her what it meant to have someone in her corner, someone who would take care of her in every way. She wouldn't have to worry about anything except being her true self.

"Do you have any bath toys?" Storm asked once they stepped into her small, cozy bathroom.

Brook pointed toward the cabinet under the sink, her cheeks pink with shyness and excitement. It pleased him more than he expected to see how prepared she was for Little Space, even without a Daddy in her life. Some Littles struggled to indulge that part of themselves without a caregiver, but she'd clearly found ways to nurture her Little side on her own. She had even proudly declared herself her own caregiver. Even if she had been doing a shit job of it. Fucking adorable.

Crouching down, Storm opened the cabinet and pulled out a small plastic bin filled with brightly colored toys— rubber ducks, boats, and a few squishy animals. His lips twitched into a rare, soft smile as he turned to her, offering the bucket to her.

The sight of her growing smaller before his eyes made his chest tighten. Giving her a bath felt so natural, like they'd been doing it for years. He filled the tub with warm water, adding a bit of bubble bath she'd shown him on the counter, and soon, the room was filled with the soft scent of cherry and vanilla.

As she climbed into the tub, her Little side took over completely. The transformation was almost magical—her giggles echoed lightly off the tiled walls as she splashed in the water, stacking her toys into towers and pushing boats across the bubbles. He knelt beside the tub, watching her as he dipped a washcloth into the warm water and began washing her.

He moved slowly and methodically, starting with her shoulders and working his way down her arms, her back, and her legs. She relaxed into his care with ease, her breathing steady and soft. But when he gently guided the washcloth between her thighs, she tensed for a moment, her breath hitching slightly. He didn't hover, didn't make a big deal out of it. Instead, he moved on quickly, respecting her space and comfort. He wanted her to stay in this peaceful headspace for the rest of the night. He thought their time in the bathroom had possibly been more personal than anything else they'd done that day.

When the water finally drained, Brook sighed heavily, her reluctance to leave her bubbles evident. Storm held out a bucket and gave her a single, stern look. "Toys, sunshine."

She pouted for a split second but obeyed, tossing her toys into the bucket one by one.

"Good girl. Come on, let's get you ready for ni-night."

Everything about the process felt easy, natural. The way she slipped her small hand into his, the trust in her wide eyes as she let him wrap her in a fluffy towel, drying her with care before selecting a pair of soft, pastel pajamas from her pink dresser. She didn't hesitate as he helped her put them on, her movements languid and sleepy, her eyes growing heavier with every passing minute.

It had been so long since Storm had gotten a Little ready for bed, but the intimacy of the moment hit him hard. It wasn't just a routine—it was a connection, a trust he hadn't realized he'd been craving or been missing. As he tucked her into bed, he knew he wanted this every night for the rest of his life. The simplicity of caring for her, of being there for her in every way, felt like a gift he wasn't sure he deserved but would fight to keep.

Once she was settled with a stuffie tucked under each arm, he sat on the edge of the bed and stared at her. He would never get tired of this sight.

"Are you too sleepy to talk about limits and rules tonight, sunshine?" he asked.

She looked sleepy, but it wasn't all that late yet.

"No, I want to talk about them," she answered. "Will you snuggle me while we talk, though?"

His pulse raced faster, and a lump formed in his throat. Fuck. When had he become such a softy over being asked to cuddle?

"Of course."

He pulled the covers back and settled next to her,

pulling her into his embrace. As soon as she wrapped herself into his arms, everything went quiet in his mind and all he felt was peace. This was perfection.

They held each other silently for a few minutes before Storm cleared his throat. "I want to know about your hard limits first, as well as any soft limits you may have."

He ran his fingers down her arm, wanting to know everything she was willing to share. A lot of things he would learn as their relationship progressed, but they needed a starting point.

"I guess I wouldn't like to be called names or be degraded. Um, I'm not sure what else. I haven't thought about it much. My ex kept things pretty basic. He didn't like experimenting."

It took a ridiculous amount of restraint not to let out a string of curse words. With every piece of new information he learned about the guy, Storm hated him more and more. That idiot did not deserve Brook.

"I can assure you, baby, I like experimenting and trying new things, but I'll never push your boundaries past what you're comfortable with. Since you haven't thought a lot about what your hard limits are, I'm going to ask about some specific things."

Brook nodded and buried herself deeper against his side. If we weren't careful, he'd get distracted and end up stripping her naked again.

"Do you have any objections to bare bottom spankings, forced orgasms, orgasm denial, being restrained, anal, or me being rough with you within reason during sex?"

She squirmed, and when he glanced down to look at

her, her cheeks were bright red. He suspected she wasn't used to having such blunt conversations.

"Um, well, orgasm denial sounds like it sucks."

He chuckled. "My question wasn't if you thought it sucked, I was asking if it's a hard limit."

"I suppose not," she muttered with a little huff. "Although denying orgasms sounds super mean."

His lips twitched. "Then I guess you better be a good girl so I won't have to resort to punishing you that way."

# TWELVE
## BROOK

Sheesh.

Talking about limits had gotten her hot and bothered despite being ridiculously comfortable in his arms. He'd listed a handful of things, which she decided wouldn't be a hard limit. When he told her she could change her mind at any time, she was relieved. Most of the things he'd said she had never tried, so she couldn't be sure if she would like them. Like anal. It intrigued her, but she'd also had Storm's cock in her pussy earlier, and that had been a stretch. She couldn't imagine him trying to fit that monster in her bottom.

Then they spent the next half hour going over her rules. He didn't give her anything unexpected. She knew what most of Carlee's rules were, and Storm's were similar for her. The only one she was mostly worried about was the strict bedtime he gave her of ten o'clock on work nights. Usually, she was just settling into bed and turning on her e-reader around that time. When she tried to argue, he said it was non-negotiable since going to bed at ten would give her eight hours of sleep before she had to wake up. Apparently when it came to her health and safety rules, he wasn't willing to budge. It was sweet, but also, part of her wanted to tell him to kick rocks because she loved reading late at night.

"Speaking of bedtimes, you're tired and need to go to sleep," he told her, sliding out from the covers.

The mattress instantly felt too cool, and she missed the quiet strength of his body.

"Are you leaving?" Her bottom lip trembled when she asked, and she hated that.

Normally, she'd be dying to get some alone time after spending an evening with another person, but she didn't want Storm to go. He didn't drain her. He seemed to understand how she functioned because he needed the quietness, too.

Storm paused, his eyebrows pinched as he looked down at her. "I don't want to overwhelm you, baby. I know you're not used to having someone around here all the time."

When she nodded but didn't say anything, he knelt on the bed and hovered over her, his gaze penetrating hers. "Tell me what you're thinking, sunshine. I can't read your mind."

She bit down on her bottom lip, not wanting to come off as too needy.

"Remember your rule about communication and honesty, Brook," he warned.

Letting out a deep breath, she ran her fingers over his tattooed arm. "I don't want you to go," she whispered, finding a short burst of courage.

He stared down at her for a moment, then rose to his full height. Panic rose in her chest. She shouldn't have said anything. Storm liked his space, too.

As she sat up to apologize and tell him it was okay, she froze because he started stripping.

"What are you doing?" she asked.

"I sleep naked, baby," is all he said as he dropped his underwear before climbing into bed next to her.

Heat rushed to her core, and her heart pounded. He was staying. She told him what she wanted, and he was actually doing it because he cared about her feelings. The big, growly, beautiful man cared about her.

That knowledge settled into her bones, and she cuddled against his warmth again. Instead of wanting to turn on her e-reader, she closed her eyes and faded to sleep within minutes.

*Three days later…*

Brook frowned at her phone, her brows pinched tightly together as she stared at the screen. This was getting ridiculous. Another unknown number. It was the third of the day, and her call log from the past two days showed an unsettling pattern—five calls yesterday, four the day before. Each time, silence greeted her on the other end.

Unease bubbled low in her stomach, twisting into a knot she couldn't ignore any longer. Her thumb hovered over the screen. A deep sigh escaped her lips as she set the phone on the table, her mind churning.

Maybe she should tell Storm. He would probably want to know. Scratch that—he would definitely want to know. He was fiercely protective, and if he caught even a whiff of something scaring her, he'd move heaven and earth to deal with it. That thought alone gave her comfort, but the last thing she wanted to do was to ruin the blissful bubble they'd been living in these past few days.

Being with him had been nothing short of amazing. Storm had effortlessly stepped into the role of her Daddy, making her feel and experience things she'd never thought possible. Each night, he had her screaming his name, his relentless focus on her pleasure leaving her trembling and thoroughly satisfied before tucking her into bed like she was the most precious thing in the world. He was demanding yet gentle, grumpy yet attentive, and so utterly perfect for her that it made her heart ache.

No, she couldn't bother him with this. She was probably overreacting anyway. It was likely just a telemarketer or some automated dialing system. Plenty of people got annoying spam calls, right? This was nothing.

Brook picked up her phone again, stared at the missed call for another long moment, and then shoved it into her purse with more force than necessary. She had far more enjoyable things to think about than random phone calls—like how Storm's gravelly voice made her shiver when he called her "sunshine" or the way his dark eyes softened every time he looked at her like she was his favorite thing in the world.

Her chest tightened as she leaned back in her chair, her lips curling into a soft smile. She was madly, completely, head-over-heels in love with Storm.

Her phone buzzed again, snapping her out of her thoughts. Another unknown number. Her stomach twisted sharply this time, and she hesitated for a beat before declining the call. She'd have to deal with this eventually, even if she had to get her number changed.

*Four days later…*

Tears threatened to spill down her cheeks.

*Another* call.

Brook picked up her phone. "Hello."

Nothing but silence on the other end.

Who was this person who kept drop calling her? Was it just a kid pranking her or someone who kept getting the wrong number?

She still hadn't told Storm she was getting these calls, and she wished she had. As soon as he got home, she was going to tell him.

*Home.*

He'd been staying her place for the past week, and it

was starting to feel like they lived together. And to her utter shock, she didn't hate it. She actually loved spending all her spare time with him.

It was only a matter of days before his house purchase closed and he got the keys, so she suspected the nights of him sleeping at her house were going to come to an end soon. The thought bugged her. It was too soon to live together, but it felt so right at the same time.

Since he was out on a group ride today and it was the weekend, she didn't have any plans, she'd stayed at her apartment and decided to curl up with a book and one of her stuffies. She hadn't gotten to read much lately because while Storm spoiled the heck out of her, he was also strict and made her go to bed at ten o'clock sharp every night. It helped that he always crawled into bed and snuggled her to sleep.

A knock on her door pulled her attention away from the spicy story she had just started. Sighing, she went to answer it. When were the neighborhood kids going to realize she wasn't interested in whatever sale they were having for their school? It seemed like every other week one of them came knocking, trying to get her to buy chocolates or wrapping paper or some other overpriced item she didn't need.

Only, when she swung the door open, she wasn't greeted by a school kid with cookies. Instead, it was a large man with a red face and a stained shirt. Her mouth went dry, and she took a step back, her tummy coiling with fear.

"Your fucking insurance company is refusing to pay for the damage to my car," he sneered, his words slightly slurred.

It took her a second to understand what he was saying. Of course they would refuse; the accident was his fault.

"I—" she started as panic surged through her.

"Shut up, bitch. You owe me a thousand bucks for the damage and that's without the stress and pain I've been in, so you better pay up because I'm not leaving until you do." He was so angry that bits of spittle flew out of his mouth.

She shook her head and moved to close the door so she could shut him out and lock it, but he stuck his foot in front of it, blocking her attempts to keep herself safe.

"I've been calling and calling, but you stopped answering, so don't try to hide from me now," he snapped, shoving the door open again.

Brook stumbled backward, her grip on the knob the only thing from making her fall.

Before she could figure out what to do next, Storm appeared behind the guy, his face in a deadly scowl. He grabbed the man by the back of his shirt and yanked him away from her, throwing him onto the ground with ease.

"What the fuck are you doing here?" Storm shouted as he stood over the guy with clenched fists.

Storm didn't give him a chance to answer before he punched him several times as the man tried to cover his already bloody face.

"Daddy!" she screamed, those threatened tears now tracking down her face.

He paused his punches and looked back at her, his expression softening just slightly.

"Go call the cops," he told her. "Go, baby, now."

She scurried inside on trembling legs and found her

phone. Sirens already blared in the distance by the time she ended the call to the 911 operator.

Yet more tears brimmed in Brook's eyes, blurring her vision as she collapsed onto the couch, her knees too weak to hold herself up any longer. When Storm's strong arms enveloped her, it was like a dam broke. The sobs she'd been holding back tumbled out as she buried her face in his chest, clinging to him like her life depended on it.

"Shh," he murmured softly, his lips brushing the crown of her head. "I got you, baby. I'm right here. He's not going to hurt you. The police are here."

He held her close, his large hands rubbing circles over her back, his grip firm but gentle, as if silently reminding her that she was safe now that he was here. Storm would always keep her safe.

When an officer walked in, Storm kept her perched on his lap, his arms a protective cage around her as she recounted what had happened. Her voice quivered, and each word felt like dragging nails across her soul. She hated admitting to receiving the unknown calls for a week, hated the weight of Storm's dark gaze on her as she confessed to hiding them from him.

The officer nodded, his expression professional but tinged with sympathy. He jotted down notes, handed her his card, and assured her they would handle it. Then, with a polite tip of his hat, he left, closing the door behind him.

The moment they were alone, the room felt suffocating. Silence stretched between them, and it felt like the walls were closing in on her. It was painful. Brook couldn't bring herself to look at him. She could *feel* the intensity of his stare without seeing it, though.

Finally, unable to bear it any longer, she risked a glance. Her heart sank at what she saw—Storm's jaw tight, his dark eyes filled with a mixture of frustration, pain, and disappointment.

"I'm sorry I didn't tell you," she whispered. "I didn't think it was a big deal."

Storm let out a dry scoff, shaking his head. His knuckles, bruised from his earlier fight, flexed as he ran a hand through his hair. "We'll deal with you disobeying a safety rule and keeping important information from me later," he said, his tone even but laced with a sharp edge. "Right now, I'm too angry to punish you, and honestly..." As his hand cupped her cheek, his next words came out softer. "I just need to hold you because I've never been so fucking scared."

Her throat tightened, fresh tears spilling down her cheeks. Sadness seeped through her, more painful than any punishment could ever be. Disappointing Storm was the last thing she *ever* wanted to do. Knowing she had killed her inside.

Without hesitation, she curled into him again, tucking her head under his chin. His arms encased her, pulling her closer as if he could shield her from everything, including her own guilt.

"I'm so sorry, Daddy," she whispered, sounding utterly broken.

His hand gently tilted her chin, forcing her to meet his gaze. The fire in his eyes had softened into something far more profound—a mix of worry, protectiveness, and an aching desire to make her understand just how much she meant to him.

"You're my sunshine, Brook. The light to my storm. I'm in love with you, and it's my privilege to be your Daddy," he said roughly. "I'll do whatever it takes to protect you. But I need you to *let* me. You have to trust me enough to tell me these things, even if you think they're small or insignificant."

She nodded, her lip trembling as his words sank in. Storm loved her. And she'd already messed up. Tears continued to drip down her face at the importance of his words despite her behavior.

"I love you too, Daddy. So much."

They stayed like that for hours, eventually dozing together on the couch. When they finally woke up, Storm led her into the bathroom.

"Go potty, then come into your room."

She nodded and did her business, nerves wracking through her.

When she returned, she sat on the edge of her bed, her fingers fidgeting with the hem of her sweater as her heart pounded against her ribcage. The atmosphere was thick with tension. When Storm joined her, he sighed and looked over, pinning her with his dark stare.

"Come here," he said finally, his tone low and steady, leaving no room for argument.

Her stomach twisted as she stood and shuffled a few steps toward him. She felt small under his gaze and not in the good, comforting way she usually did when they were in their dynamic. This was different. She'd disappointed him, and that knowledge settled painfully in her chest. She never wanted to feel like this ever again.

When she stopped in front of him, he reached out, taking her hands in his.

"Do you know why we're here right now, sunshine?" he asked, tilting his head slightly as he waited for her response.

She nodded quickly, her throat dry. "Because I broke a safety rule," she breathed.

"That's right," he said, his thumb brushing over her knuckles. "And what's the most important thing about our relationship?"

"That I'm honest with you... so you can keep me safe."

"Exactly." His eyes softened just a fraction, but his tone remained firm. "By not telling me about those calls, you put yourself in danger, Brook. If I had known, I would have investigated and probably figured out that it was that asshole. Could have had a restraining order put in place or had him arrested for harassing you. Do you understand that?"

New tears welled up in her eyes. "I'm sorry, Daddy. I really am. I didn't think it was that big of a deal."

"Sunshine," he said softly, his thumb now tracing slow, soothing circles on the back of her hand. "It's *my* job to decide what's a big deal when it comes to your safety. Not yours. I can't protect you if I don't know what's going on."

She swallowed hard and nodded, those welling tears threatening to spill over. "I won't do it again."

"I know you won't, baby," he replied. "But tonight, you're going to get a spanking to remind you why safety rules aren't optional. Understand?"

Her breath hitched, her heart racing. She nodded, unable to find the words to reply.

"Words, sunshine." He waited, raising his eyebrows.

"Yes, Daddy."

"Good girl." He gave her hands a reassuring squeeze before guiding her around to his side.

Then he guided her over his lap, not wasting any time as he lowered her leggings and panties to her thighs. She whimpered but didn't fight him because she deserved this. More than that, she was pretty sure she *needed* this.

Storm's hand rested lightly on her lower back for a moment. "What's your safeword?"

"Red,"

"And you'll use it if you need me to stop?"

"Yes, Daddy."

"Good girl."

The first swat landed on her bottom, the sharp sound echoing in the quiet room. She gasped, her fingers curling into the thick comforter on her bed. He gave her a moment to process before delivering another, then another. She wiggled against his hold, kicking her feet slightly as he spanked her over and over again.

Tears raced down her cheeks as he picked up speed. Her bottom and tops of her thighs were on fire. Finally, he stopped, and she let out a deep breath.

"Why are your safety rules important?" he asked, his large hand rubbing her sore, hot bottom.

"Because they help you keep me safe," she whimpered.

"That's right, baby. I love you, and I need you to remember that."

The pain of this spanking was nothing in comparison to the way she felt over disappointing him. In the short time they'd been together, Storm had been an amazing Daddy, and she'd let him down.

"I'm sorry, Daddy."

"I accept your apology, sunshine, and once this spanking is over, you're completely forgiven. Once this is done, we move on and leave it in the past. Understood?"

She sniffled and nodded. "Yes, Daddy."

"Good. The rest of this is going to be hard and fast," he warned as he shifted and lowered one of his legs over both of hers so she couldn't kick out.

Without warning, he started spanking her so hard it stole the breath from her lungs, and she struggled against his hold.

"Owwie!" she cried, a sob escaping her lips.

He didn't stop for what felt like forever. Not until she finally gave in to it and went limp over his lap, her entire body shaking with sob after agonized sob.

He delivered two final swats, then gently rubbed her back. "All done, baby. It's over. Come here. All is forgiven."

Storm helped her up and pulled her into his arms. She buried her face in his chest and carried on crying both from the stinging of her bottom and the fear of what could have happened if her Daddy hadn't shown up when he did. His arms wrapped around her tightly, holding her close as he murmured soothing words into her hair.

"You're my good girl, Brook. Always. This doesn't change that."

Her heart swelled at his words, the guilt easing slightly as she clung to him. She felt safe again, cherished and loved despite her mistake. And she silently vowed never to break another safety rule again.

# THIRTEEN
## STORM

Ever since her spanking had ended a few hours before, Brook had been extra clingy, and if he were totally honest, he loved it. He had slipped her pacifier into her mouth as he comforted her afterward, and she'd been using it on and off since.

After feeding her, he'd gotten her changed into some cute pink pajamas and they'd crawled into bed to watch a movie.

His heart had stopped the moment he'd seen that asshole in Brook's doorway. He couldn't even think about what the fucker might have done to her if he hadn't got there when he did. Storm hoped he was in a jail cell getting his ass kicked already because the fucker deserved way more than what Storm gave him. If Brook hadn't been there, he might have killed the guy, but Storm didn't want to traumatize his Little girl more than she already was.

"Baby," he said gently.

She looked up at him, her eyes still slightly puffy from

all her crying. When she gave him a soft, sweet smile, he melted. One day, he was going to marry her. He didn't need a year or more to know that. They belonged together, and that was all there was to it.

"Move in with me when I get the keys to the house."

Asking was probably the right thing to do, but Storm had never been one to ask. If he wanted something, he got it. Although if it came down to it, he'd get on his knees and fucking beg Brook to live with him in his new house. Their new *home*.

When she didn't say anything right away, his chest tightened. *Fuck.*

Then a smile spread over her face, and she reached up to run her fingers over the scruff of his beard. "Okay."

His eyebrows shot up. "Yeah?"

"Are you sure you want someone around all the time? Didn't you want to buy the house so you could get some quiet time?"

"I think the real reason I bought the house was that it was too fucking painful to see my friends find the love of their lives and I was alone. I didn't realize I was lonely until I met you. You're it for me, sunshine. I've never been more sure about anything in my life."

As much as he had enjoyed his alone time, he loved being around Brook even more. She was the sunshine he needed.

"Okay," she whispered. "Let's do it."

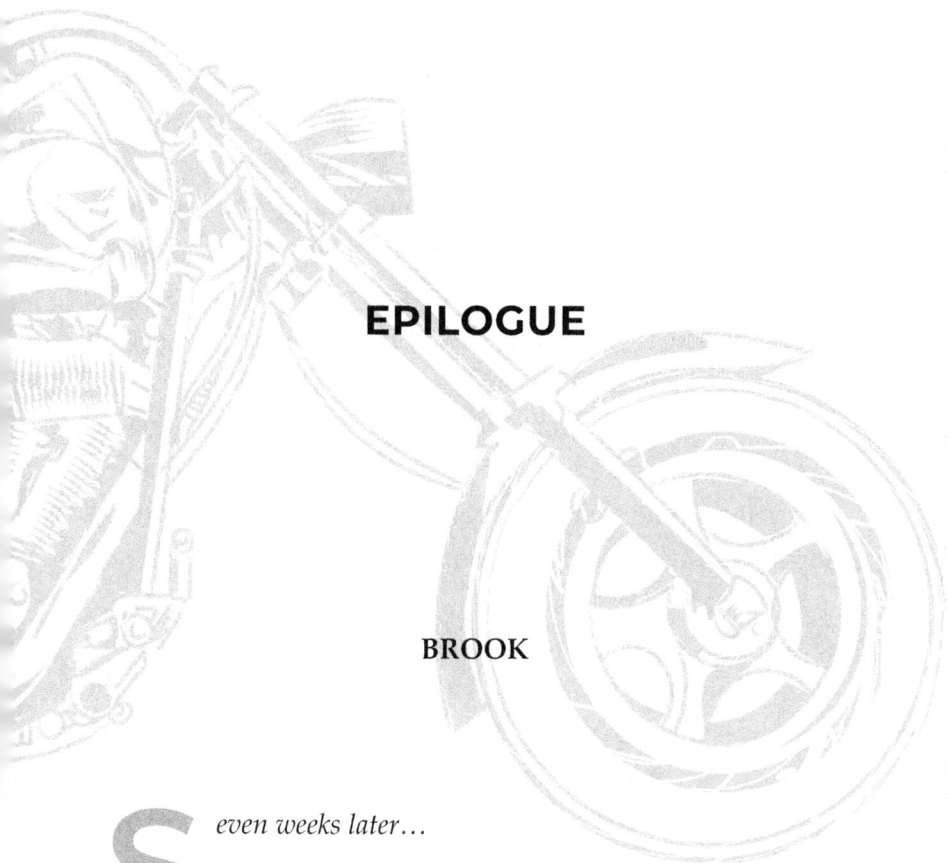

# EPILOGUE

## BROOK

S*even weeks later...*

"No running, sunshine!"

*Whoops.*

One would think she'd have learned by now. In the past six weeks, she'd gotten in trouble more times than she could count for running through the house. It was just so easy to do. The wide hallways and open living room gave Brook all the space she could possibly want to run, skip, and hop through the beautiful hardwood-floored home.

"Sorry, Daddy!" she called back as she skidded to a halt in front of the front door.

After a quick check through the peephole, which she'd also learned a hard lesson about using, she swung the door open to reveal some of her very best friends. Their Daddies lingered behind them, looking lovingly at their Little girls. It was the same way Storm looked at her. As if she was his entire world and the best thing to ever happen to him.

"Brook!" Carlee squealed at the same time as Brook screamed hers.

Carlee, Eden, Remi, Harper, and Brook shared a group hug before she invited everyone inside.

She and Storm had been living together since he'd gotten the keys six weeks ago, and tonight they were hosting their first BBQ.

"I can't believe how beautiful this place is," Remi commented. "Are you sure Storm picked it out himself?"

Storm scoffed as he strode into the entryway, though an easy smile played at his lips. The man was still grumpy and growly, one of the things Brook loved so much, about him but he was smiling more and more with each passing day.

"I have excellent taste, brat," he told Remi, keeping his eyes fixed on Brook.

Remi stuck her tongue out at him and giggled, getting a swat from Kade behind her.

"What happens to Little girls who stick their tongue out?" Kade asked her.

The way Remi's cheeks turned bright pink was adorable, and Brook had to cover her mouth with her hand to hide the grin spreading across her face. She'd never get tired of the playful banter between the Daddies and the Littles. Of course, in her opinion, the Littles were much better at it.

"Can I show them my playroom, Daddy?" Brook asked Storm.

She already knew she could. She'd asked him half a dozen times as they prepared for the BBQ, but Brook was just so excited to show them what her Daddy had created for her.

"Yes," Storm replied, wrapping his hand around the back of her neck before they could take off. "But if I catch you running again tonight, we'll be making a *special* trip to our bedroom. Are we clear?"

Offering a bright, innocent smile, Brook bobbed her head. "Crystal clear, Daddy. No running. Got it. Check and check."

He narrowed his gaze and arched one of his stern eyebrows. "Being sassy isn't a good idea for the protection of your bottom, either, sunshine."

Sheesh. He was awfully strict. And she absolutely loved it. It was rare she went a full day without getting her bottom warmed, but she wouldn't want it any other way.

"Sorry, Daddy," she murmured.

"Good girl." He leaned down and pressed a kiss to her forehead, then gave her a firm swat as she turned to lead the other girls upstairs.

"That's a spare bathroom over there," she pointed to one of the first doors on the second landing. "Then there's a guest room, and across from that is Daddy's office. At the end of the hall is my playroom and then next to it is our bedroom."

Her friends peeked in each doorway, making squeals of excitement as they took it all in. Most of the house was already furnished, though they still had some things to add.

After they moved in, Storm and some of his friends had painted the entire place, changing the interior from a gross brown to a rich cream that she loved. The only room that wasn't that color was her special room.

When they got to the last door, she pushed it open and stepped in, beaming proudly. She'd had nothing to do with the décor or paint. That had all been her Daddy, but he'd totally nailed it.

"Oh my gosh, I love the pink walls," Remi gasped as she looked around. "And the bed, it's made for a princess."

It really was. Between the white metal frame and the tulle hanging from the ceiling, creating a sheer curtain, it was magical. And even though she never slept in it, she'd turned it into her favorite place to read.

Carlee instantly went to the bookshelves set up in the corner and scanned through the books. On the floor in front of them was a large beanbag with fuzzy blankets and pillows situated on it. That was Brook's second favorite place to read.

"This is the biggest Barbie house I've ever seen," Harper whispered, her eyes wide as she took in the waist-high doll house.

"Daddy had it custom-made. Isn't it perfect?"

She watched as her friends walked around, taking everything in and complimenting her on all of it . The past six weeks, her love for her Daddy grew more and more because every detail he'd put into it had been so thoughtful and completely spot on.

Carlee sniffled, and when Brook turned to look at her friend, she froze because there were tears pooling in her eyes.

"What's wrong?" Brook asked, concerned.

"Nothing. I'm just so happy for you," Carlee explained, wiping her cheek. "You look so happy, and so does Storm. I miss him living at the clubhouse, but after seeing all of this, I'm thrilled for both of you."

A lump formed in Brook's throat. She stepped forward and wrapped her arms around her closest friend, squeezing her tightly.

"I never would have found the Daddy of my dreams if it weren't for you, Carlee. Thank you for introducing us."

The two girls embraced each other for a long moment, only pulling away when Storm appeared. "Appetizers are ready," he announced.

His gaze zeroed in on them, concern etched on his face. "What's wrong?" he asked.

Shaking her head, Brook went to him and slid her hands around his waist, clinging to him. "Nothing, Daddy. They're happy tears."

Carlee and the other Littles filed out of the beautiful room, leaving the two of them alone.

"Happy tears?"

She nodded. "Yeah, Daddy. Thank you for giving me everything I could have ever hoped for."

He studied her for a second, his Adam's apple bobbing as he swallowed. When he finally spoke, his voice was rough. "I should be the one thanking you, sunshine.

You've given me a purpose in life. A reason to breathe. I was just a shell before I met you."

They held each other for a few minutes until her tears dried, and then he took her by the hand and led her out of the perfect room.

"Let's go entertain our friends, baby girl."

Nodding, she followed him downstairs. Before they entered the kitchen, Storm stopped and turned toward her. "Don't even *think* about starting a food fight with the cake tonight. Understood?"

Warmth spread through her as her tummy fluttered with excitement. Offering him an innocent smile, she lifted a shoulder. "I wouldn't even consider doing something like that, Daddy. I don't know why you'd think so."

His dark gaze pierced right through her. "Uh huh. This is your only warning, Little girl."

"'Kay, Daddy."

After studying her with a weary expression for a few seconds, he turned and they continued to the kitchen.

As soon as they rounded the corner, Brook met Carlee's gaze, grinning at each other with mischief written all over their faces before glancing at the cake sitting on the counter. She couldn't be positive, but Brook was pretty sure her best friend was thinking the same thing as her.

It was going to be a good night.

Icing and all.

And the fun would totally be worth the spanking that would follow.

Because Brook knew no matter how naughty she was, how moody she was, how much of an introvert she was, her Daddy would love her through it all.

"Daddy," she whispered.

He glanced down at her and wrapped a protective arm around her shoulders. "Yeah, sunshine?"

"I love you."

Without pause or hesitation, Storm cupped her chin and lowered his mouth to hers. "I love you, too, baby. With all my heart."

And even though she felt the same way, she knew she'd love him even more tomorrow.

"Let's raise a toast," Storm announced.

Everyone gathered around the gleaming kitchen island, some holding beer bottles while others had sippy cups. It was an odd mix of drinks, yet it was perfect for the Shadowridge Guardians.

"To friends who have become family and Little girls who make our lives better." Storm kept his gaze on her as he spoke. "Cheers."

"Cheers!"

Then, one by one, they all tapped their drinks together.

"To us," Storm whispered in her ear.

She grinned up at him, her heart squeezing so tight. "To us, Daddy, forever."

# ALSO BY KATE OLIVER

**West Coast Daddies Series**

Ally's Christmas Daddy

Haylee's Hero Daddy

Maddie's Daddy Crush

Safe With Daddy

Trusting Her Daddy

Ruby's Forever Daddies

**Daddies of the Shadows Series**

Knox

Ash

Beau

Wolf

Leo

Maddox

Colt

Hawk

Angel

Tate

**Rawhide Ranch**

A Little Fourth of July Fiasco

**Shadowridge Guardians**

(A multi-author series)

Kade

Doc

**Syndicate Kings**

Corrupting Cali: Declan's Story

Saving Scarlet: Killian's Story

Controlling Chloe: Bash's Story

Possessing Paisley: Kieran's Story

Keeping Katie: Grady's Story

Taking Tessa: Ronan's Story

**Daddies of Pine Hollow**

Jaxon

Dane

Nash

**Dark Ops Daddies**

Cage

Jasper

# KEEP UP WITH KATE!

Sign up for my newsletter get teasers, cover reveals, updates, and extra content!

SCAN ME TO SIGN UP NOW!

# THE KINDEST THING YOU CAN DO FOR AN AUTHOR IS TO LEAVE A POSITIVE REVIEW!

Printed in Great Britain
by Amazon